Two Decades Apart

Theresa A. Moseley PhD

ISBN-13: 978-1-7351126-1-9

For information regarding special discounts for bulk purchases, please contact the publisher: LaBoo Publishing Enterprise, LLC
staff@laboopublishing.com
www.laboopublishing.com

Printed in the United States of America

Dedication

I dedicate this book to my father, the late SFC
Clarence B. Moseley. I love you!

Acknowledgments

I would like to acknowledge several people who have inspired and supported me through the years. First, my dad was my biggest cheerleader. He was one of the smartest men I've known, a former Airborne Ranger with a gentle spirit. He was a true Pisces. I get all of my creative gifts from my dad. Col. Samuel H. Whitley, my company commander in Sinop, Turkey, was the first person other than my dad who told me I was brilliant and could do anything in this world I put my mind to. He recognized my talents and assured me that whatever I decided to do long term, I would be successful. I'd like to thank my life-long friends, Dorothy Stewart, Cheryl Marrow, Joyce Boone, and my Savoy Heights crew, for their uncon-ditional love and always being here for me. I have friends I've known for 57 years from Savoy Heights in Fayetteville, NC. Although I have not lived there since 1976, we still communicate and support one another in all our endeavors. I am eternally grateful to Dr. Tasheka Green for introducing me to Kimmoly LaBoo, my publisher, while collaborating on *Women of Virtue Walking in Excellence.* I already had the vision to write this love story; however, Kimmoly gave me the perseverance to finish it. Last, I'd like to thank God for answering my prayers and guiding me in the right direction to let me know that I am living in my purpose, but I have more work to do. I learned early in life that writing was cathartic for me. Through the ongoing support of my family and friends, I will continue to share love, peace, and hope through my writings.

Preface

This love story about a woman and a man who were born two decades apart is told over four seasons. They are looking for their divine purpose after they both had near-death experiences. They meet during their travels and decide to explore the world together. Their mutual love for music, art and world peace brings them together. The love story, expressed through the sensual feelings that they have for one another, is felt through the music, scenery, and thoughts. This allows the reader to determine what the physical connection would be.

They are highly successful people in their career fields, as well as philanthropists and humanitarians. Their stories address many problems in society today, such as school violence, police brutality, teen pregnancy, diabetes, heart disease and cancer. Throughout the love story, these obstacles are overcome by faith, hope, and love. Eva is an altruistic person who doesn't wait for someone to ask for assistance. She already knows what everyone needs. Her intuitiveness is a special trait that she uses to help others. She is very spiritual and meditates daily.

Aaron is an eminent, gifted musician. He's played the piano since he was five years old. He shares his world with his best friend Rhondell, his old college roommate and an impressionist artist. The fraternity brotherhood is close and they see the world through the same lens.

Eva's best friend Gina has a tough job as a high school principal; however, her friendship with Eva provides her with a resource to help her students. Eva is committed to improving the culture of Gina's school by addressing the problems in the community and how they impact the behaviors of students in the school. Eva recognizes the perverse behaviors of some of the students and provides group counseling sessions to get clarity on the real issues at hand.

The story connects two families, the O'Sullivans and the Kellys. They come together for every holiday and create their own traditions. The main characters travel from Canada to Australia, South America and Europe as they grow to love each other more and more. The theme of *two decades apart* is revealed in several relationships: Eva and Aaron, Ursula and Nicolette, and Daisy and Eva. Each chapter intertwines with the next as relationships and personal experiences come together to reveal their divine purpose in life.

Chapter 1

Eva Whitfield O'Sullivan is a 50-year-old college professor who lives on a lake near Seattle, Washington. She is a petite woman, five foot four, with a small frame. Eva was an athlete in high school and college and has maintained her athletic build. Her hair is long and black and her eyes are dark brown. Her skin is the color of coffee with cream and her face is timeless. She is a natural beauty and does not wear a lot of makeup. She wears designer clothes, mostly in neutral colors, and drives a luxury car. She has a scar on her leg from a childhood accident while swinging. Eva is a spiritual woman who has a lot of faith. She prays before every meal and when she wakes up and goes to sleep. She also has a meditation room where she meditates every day. Eva exercises daily and has a morning ritual of drinking tea and listening to Tchaikovsky. Eva is always helping others. It doesn't matter whether she knows the person or not. Eva will help a stranger crossing the street, donate to charities, and speak at charity events. She loves motivational speaking and sending a message of love and hope.

She has a personal assistant and housekeeper, Maria Sanchez, who keeps her busy life on track. Maria knows everything Eva needs and wants. Every morning she makes Eva a cup of Earl Grey tea and places the pot on the patio overlooking the lake. It's often raining in the morning and Eva enjoys the drizzle and watching the rain hit the lake and hearing it hit the tin roof that covers her patio. Maria provides Eva with a list of things to do for the day and reminds her to call her best friend Gina Newton to see what time she wants her to speak to a group of students at Sanford High School where Gina is the principal. "Of course! I didn't forget Gina. By the way, I have something for you." Eva pulls out an envelope and gives it to Gina. It is a day spa treatment.

"This is for me?"

"Of course! You do so much for me, you need a break. Enjoy yourself."

Maria says, "You are the best boss in the world. Thank you, Eva. I love you."

Chapter 2

Robert and Helen O'Sullivan adopted Eva the day she was born. Robert was six foot two, with a lean body. He was retired from the Army and spent his days on the golf course. He had a great since of humor and talked with his hands a lot. His wife Helen was short and petite. She golfed with her husband and spent the rest of her time reading and shopping. She had always been a stay-at-home mom; however, she had a degree in accounting which she used during tax season. She worked in that field until she was 60.

Eva's birth mother was from Salters, South Carolina. Daisy Baptiste Whitfield was a retired attorney and judge. Daisy wanted to continue to work well into her 70s but due to her illnesses, diabetes and heart disease, she retired early. Daisy was married and enrolled in college when her husband suddenly died in a car accident. Three weeks later she discovered they were expecting a child. Daisy knew she could not continue college and take care of a baby full time. She wanted the best for her child and believed that letting her best friends adopt and raise Eva was the best choice. Daisy asked the O'Sullivans to adopt Eva but she wanted them to guarantee three things. "First, I want to name her Eva Whitfield O'Sullivan. Second, when I pass the bar and get a job, I want to take care of her financially. Last, if she ever needs anything or wants to meet me, let her know I will be there for her and yes, I will meet her when the time comes."

Daisy Whitfield never married again and did not have any more children. She graduated from law school and went on to become a well-known lawyer and judge. Daisy made sure she had a living trust for Eva. She kept her promise and took care of Eva financially. The O'Sullivans made sure that Eva knew her birth mother loved her and took care of her.

The O'Sullivans, who could not have children, were more than happy to adopt Eva, as they loved Daisy Whitfield and would do anything for her. Eva was their only child and they provided her with the best education and life. Eva had piano lessons, ballet lessons, tennis lessons, and loved classical music. Eva played the violin and flute in band in high school. She also loved art and had a nice collection. Eva had lots of friends growing up. They were always curious about her Irish last name. Eva told them her father's father was Irish but she was adopted. She didn't know her real father. One day Eva came home from middle school and asked her mother about her biological father. Eva's mother went into her closet and pulled out an old photo album. There were lots of clothes hanging in the walk-in closet but one white bag stood out. Eva asked her mom what was in that bag. Ms. O'Sullivan told her, "One day, you will find out."

Eva said, "Of course you won't tell me now."

Her mother smiled as she pulled the photo album down. They walked to the sunroom arm in arm as Helen continued to talk about Eva's dad, Anthony Gaskins. Her mother turned to a page where there were a man and a woman standing next to a '59 Chevy Impala.

Helen O'Sullivan began to tell the story of Daisy Whitfield and Anthony Gaskins. "Your mother knew your father for 20 years. They grew up together. They went to the same school and both went to college to study law. Your parents married during their sophomore year of college. One day Anthony was going to a flower shop to get Daisy some flowers. It was no special occasion… he was just a romantic and chivalrous kind of guy. Anthony was very articulate and had a lot of charisma. He was such a sesquipedalian and would have been an incredible lawyer. Your mom used to love to hear him talk and lecture. He used to write your mother love letters too, comparing his love to her with the heat burning in the Sahara Desert. She used to share them with me. I was jealous because Robert, who was in Officers' Candidate School never had time to do those special things." Eva smiled and listened intently. "Anthony was driving his '59 Chevy Impala when he was hit by a drunk driver. He died instantly. Your mother was so devastated. She cried for months. She stayed with us after she found out she was expecting you. We made her feel welcome and comfortable. Every week she visited your dad's grave. She promised him that you would have a good life and the best of everything. She promised him that you would receive the best education and be somebody in this world. She really loved him." Helen laughed, "It's interesting!! She really loved him but did not take his last name of Gaskins. She said she did not like his last name. Sounded too much like gas can." They both laughed.

"That can't be the real reason," said Eva.

"Daisy had always been a feminist. She loved him dearly but being her authentic self, she kept her last name." The Whitfields have a long history in South Carolina. When you are ready, I'll give you that history lesson."

Eva hugged her mother and said, "Wow! I wonder who else is in this book of pictures that I need to know. I love you, Mom!" Finally, Eva knew a little more about her real mom and dad. Eva always remembered the conversation she had with her mom in middle school. Sometimes she would daydream about her parents.

Years passed and Eva was now an adult, well known in her community as a humanitarian and a tenured college professor of psychology.

Chapter 3

On a normal rainy day in Seattle, Washington Eva Whitfield O'Sullivan got in her car to drive to work at the university. She waved goodbye to her personal assistant and drove down the driveway. As she drove down the picturesque highway she turned on her favorite classical work, Tchaikovsky's Symphony No. 6, the Pathetique. As the first few bars played Eva smiled. All of a sudden the music stopped. There was silence. Eva was suddenly standing in bright light and a field of flowers. The colors were so bright and beautiful, she just stood in awe. Suddenly she saw a man with a familiar face. She did not know who he was but his face was familiar.

The next thing Eva heard was a voice saying, "Hang in there, Eva. You are going to be okay." Eva opened her eyes and two paramedics were asking her where she hurt. Eva realized that she must have been in an accident. In fact, she was hit by a truck that lost control on the wet highway while she was on her way to work. The police found Eva's identification and called her parents. Eva's dad told the police to take his daughter to the best trauma hospital in the area. Eva's parents rushed to the hospital to be by their daughter's side.

Eva was unconscious when she arrived at the hospital. She flat-lined twice; however, each time, she was revived. X-rays showed no internal injuries to major organs in the trunk of her body; however, her brain was swelling as fluid built up around her brain. Eva had a series of ultrasounds, MRI scans, and CT scans that revealed she had hydrocephalus. The doctors knew the head trauma from the accident was causing the problem. A ventriculostomy was performed to allow the cerebrospinal fluid (CSF) to leave her brain.

Helen O'Sullivan called Daisy Whitfield to inform her of her daughter's accident. She was in a coma now and the doctors said it could go either way. Daisy was 69 years old now and in poor health. She walked with a cane and the circulation in her legs was poor. Helen told Daisy she would get her a private plane to Seattle. Robert called one of his army friends, Colonel Robert Hawkins, who lived in Columbia, SC and owned a private jet. His son, Pete Hawkins, was a pilot and agreed to pick up Daisy from Salters and drive her to the airfield in Columbia.

Daisy told her housekeeper that if anything happened to her, she was to give a blue box to Eva. "I know my daughter will survive. I'm not sure how much longer I have, but my daughter will survive. I need to let her know that her time on earth is not finished. She has a divine purpose to fill."

As Daisy walked out of her mansion, Pete took her luggage and walked her to the car. Daisy stopped and looked at her housekeeper standing in the door. She looked at the lake behind her house. She looked at the trees in the yard with the gray moss hanging down. She looked to her right, where she saw the headstones of the Whitfield family plot. She told Pete, "I'm ready."

Daisy Whitfield arrived at the hospital and took the elevator to Eva's room. Helen was with her but stayed behind in the waiting room. This was the first time Daisy had seen Eva since she was born. She'd seen pictures of her growing up and videos of her playing sports over the years. She smiled at her daughter, who was lying peacefully in bed. She rubbed her hair and whispered in her ear, "I love you, Eva. Eva… It's not your time. Eva, you need to wake up and live your life. Find your purpose, baby. I love you." Daisy reached in her bag and pulled out a phone. She turned some music on, and placed ear plugs in Eva's ear. Suddenly Symphony No. 6, the Pathetique, played in Eva's ear. Daisy looked at Eva, kissed her on her forehead and walked away with her cane. As soon as Daisy left, Eva opened her eyes. Daisy left the next day on the plane back to Columbia. During the car ride back to Salters, she crossed the railroad tracks and saw the old family store, post office, and shoeshine store, Daisy said, "I'm home now. Everything is going to be okay."

Chapter 4

In less than a month, Eva had a full recovery from the accident. She was home with her personal assistant, who made sure Eva took her meds and ate healthy. When she was in the hospital she was diagnosed as a Type II diabetic and with high cholesterol. Maria said, "Eva, don't forget you need to continue to exercise every day now and hold back on those carbs. If you get hungry eat more protein."

Eva was walking on the treadmill and thanking God for her life. She realized how lucky she was to be alive. Eva asked Maria, "Who played the music for me in the hospital? How did they know my favorite song? Maria, did I die?"

Maria told Eva, "You flat-lined twice in the hospital. We called your birth mother and she came to see you."

Eva's eyes opened wide. "That was my mother? I knew someone was there. She helped me. She told me it wasn't my time. Maria... I think I went to heaven… a couple of times… I kept running into a man with a familiar face. Everything was so beautiful… I wanted to stay but I guess I couldn't. It wasn't my time."

Eva looked out the window in her home. She walked to the deck overlooking the beautiful landscaping of her property. Eva said a prayer, thanking God for saving her life and giving her a chance to find out her divine purpose. "Maria… I'm going to take a sabbatical. I've got to find out why I survived. What is my purpose in life?"

Maria said, "I think you are living your purpose. You are a humanitarian and a motivational speaker, and your heart is kind and gentle. Everyone loves you as soon as they meet you."

"Maria, you are too kind. I love you!"

"I love you too. A sabbatical for you means a sabbatical for me!" They both laughed. Maria says, "Perhaps you will find a boyfriend during your travels."

Eva protested, "Maria, I date!!"

Maria replied, "Yes! That's all you do. It's not the same." They both laughed.

Eva turned her head slightly and asked, "What are you insinuating?"

Maria sipped her tea. "You know what I'm talking about."

Eva said with her chin on her left shoulder, "Perhaps!"

Maria shook her head and walked away.

Helen O'Sullivan came by to visit her daughter with a big bouquet of flowers. "Wow... Daisy came to see me." Eva welcomed her mom at the door. "I want to go see her. I want to get to know her and more about our family history. I also want to thank her for bringing the music to me. How did she know I liked...?"

Helen smiled, "I called her when you were in the hospital. She wanted to be there for you. Although she is frail now, nothing could stop her from seeing you. Your dad hired his best friend's son Pete Hawkins to fly her out here. She loves you very much." Helen O'Sullivan remembered her promise to Daisy. *Whenever she wants to see me, just let me know.* "Your mother is not in good health, so sooner is better than later."

Eva said, "I will go see her. First, I'm going to take a break and travel. I've got to figure out why I survived. What is my purpose in life? Why am I here? I feel like there is so much more I need to do in life. I'll figure it out. When I return, I'm going to Salters, SC to visit my mother."

Eva talked to her mom for a while and then she went into her meditation room. She sat down on a mat and began to pray.

"Maria! I need to plan a trip to Canada. My friends told me the Montreal Jazz Festival is excellent every year. This year they have some amazing artists. I want to go for the entire festival."

"Okay Eva. I got it."

"Oh, be sure to book a couple of days in Quebec City for me. I've never been there and I heard it's beautiful."

"No problem. You can take the train to Quebec City from Montreal. You are going to enjoy this trip. I wish I could join you."

"Okay, book two flights. Come on!"

"No, I've got plenty of work to do. Enjoy yourself."

"I wonder what the weather will be like. Hopefully no rain. Most of the concerts are outdoors. What a great way to start the summer."

Chapter 5

During the last week of June Eva arrived at the Montreal International Jazz Festival. Eva decided to make this her first stop on her tour of the world. She left Seattle, WA to fly to Montreal, Canada. She checked in at the host hotel. There were concerts all day outside near the hotel and at several other venues nearby. One evening she went to a show and a piano player caught her eye. During his solo, she was impressed with his musicality.

Eva met several people in Montreal at the hotel lobby bar who were from Seattle. Dan and Kiki Cook were a couple of musicians who attended the jazz festival every year. They told Eva that she would love the side trip to Quebec City. It was a beautiful place to visit and had some exciting tours. When Dan and Kiki left the bar, Eva saw that Kiki left her book bag. It was a few minutes after they left. Eva took the book bag to the front desk and told the receptionist the name of the guest. She left a note on the bag saying it was a pleasure to meet them.

Eva walked around the venue for the jazz festival, wondering if she would see the piano player again. There was something special about him. She stopped at a restaurant for lunch and ordered a drink. The server asked for her ID. "Really?" Eva said.

"We card everyone. I'm sorry, ma'am."

Eva showed the server her ID. "You are 50 years old?" The server looked shocked. "What is your secret?" The server smiled at Eva while shaking her head.

"I meditate and pray on a daily basis. I don't have too many vices."

"Well, you look amazing. Enjoy your lunch." Eva overheard the server talking about her little girl and how she really wanted to take piano lessons. The server could not afford it but she said she was saving her tips to make it happen. Eva listened to the conversation and smiled. Eva decided to leave the server a huge tip.

When Eva walked out the door, the server picked up the check and ran to the door. "Ma'am, you made a mistake on the tip. There're too many zeros."

"Nope, I didn't make a mistake. That's your tip. God bless you." Eva walked away.

The server was in shock and looked amazed at what had just happened. Eva loved giving and donated to several charities. She always supported local charities and she donated funds annually to a foundation that helped children go to college that could not otherwise afford to. Eva was the quintessential altruistic woman.

Eva rode the train to Quebec City, where Maria had booked a two-day stay at the Chateau Frontenac. As Eva was checking into the hotel, she saw a familiar face. It was the piano player she saw in Montreal. He was sitting in the lobby with a note pad writing. She noticed he was tall and lean with lots of muscles. His skin was brown and smooth and his eyes were light brown. His hair was cut short and his beard was groomed. His arms seemed very long and for a moment she thought about what it would be like to have those arms wrapped around her. *What am I thinking? I don't even know this man.* She smiled and kept on walking to the concierge's desk. That night Eva dreamed about the strange man she saw in the lobby and in Montreal.

She booked a tour of the city, including a boat cruise, city tour, and Montmorency Falls. Eva was enjoying listening to the tour guide, who spoke in English and French. Eva spoke French too and enjoyed ordering her food in French. Eva soaked up the French charm of Old Quebec and visited the Plains of Abraham, Place Royale, Place d'Armes and Montmorency Falls.

When she arrived at the falls she saw the man of her dreams again. He was sitting and writing as the water fell from the falls. Eva wondered why she kept running into this young man. Finally, she decided to speak. "Hi. I'm Eva!"

The young man looked up. "I'm Aaron. Aaron Kelly."

"You know... I saw you playing the piano in Montreal a few days ago. And I also saw you in my hotel today."

"Are you staying at the Chateau Frontenac?"

"Yes!" Eva was a little star struck. Aaron was about six two, two hundred twenty pounds. Eva said to herself, *You are built like a wide receiver.* Eva and Aaron had an awkward moment of silence until she said, "Did you play sports in high school?" Eva was new at the dating game so she just brought up a subject that she thought most guys would be interested in.

"Yes. High school and college. I was a wide receiver in football."

Eva laughed.

"What's so funny?"

She laughed again. "Ummm, I love football. So how long have you been playing the piano?"

Aaron lowered his head and then looked back up at Eva, "Since I was five. When I was five, I almost died from cancer. I had rigorous treatments that worked. The week before Christmas I learned I was in remission. During one of my hospital stays I met a musician who played the piano. His daughter was terminally ill with cancer. Before she died I wrote her a poem. Her father made it a song. He performed it at her funeral. I was so amazed how he took my words and placed music with it. I told my mom if I lived, that's what I wanted to do—write music and play music. I survived and here I am. Writing and playing music all over the world." He looked at the falls. "Interesting… I still don't think I've found my divine purpose." He looked at Eva. "I never told anyone that story." Aaron crosses his arms and puts his hands on his cheek. "So what brings you to Canada?"

Eva said, "Aaron, right?" She wanted to make sure she got his name right. "I was in a really bad car accident a couple of months ago and I think I died, but they brought me back. Well… Someone brought me back. It wasn't my time. I'm a college professor on sabbatical and I and looking for my divine purpose. It's amazing how much we have in common. I love music. Classical music is my favorite. Every morning I awake to Tchaikovsky."

Aaron smiled. "You are interesting. And beautiful. I hate to use this cliché, but what's your sign?"

Eva laughed and raised her eyebrows. "Pisces!"

Aaron smiled. "Me too."

Eva said, "March 2nd."

Aaron gasped, "March 3rd."

Eva grinned. "1968"

Aaron said. "1980." He looked at Eva. "Wait. What? You are not 50!!"

Eva flicked her hair back and stared in Aaron's eyes. "I am not kidding. I am 50. We are two decades apart."

Aaron said, "Not quite."

"Umm, 12 years apart."

"Well, that's not two decades."

They both laughed.

Chapter 6

Aaron had a concert at the Concert Centre Videotron in Quebec. He invited Eva to come to the show. After the show, they walked the streets of Quebec City holding hands as if they had known each other for years. Eva told Aaron about her life and Aaron shared his life story. Aaron was from Charleston, SC. His father was a real estate agent in Savannah, Georgia and his mother was a retired school teacher who lived in New York City. They divorced when he was 18. They had troubles long before then but did not want to separate while Aaron was still in high school. Although they were divorced, they remained friends. His best friend's name was Rondell Rogers, a rapper, artist, and poet. He often traveled to see Aaron perform. Aaron told Eva his mother was two years older than his dad.

Eva told Aaron, "I'm two decades older than you."

"So here's the thing: Your age doesn't matter to me."

She quickly changed the subject. "My best friend is Gina Newton. She is a high school principal. We should introduce Rondell to her."

Aaron said, "We just met and now you are hooking up my best friend?

"Touché"

"Let's change the subject. I want to hear more about your family."

"Well, my mother is Helen O'Sullivan. She was a stay-at-home mom. My dad was an officer in the Army. A lot of times we did not travel with him. My mom wanted me to have a good education and life-long friends. She wasn't into moving every three years. As a result, I am very close to her. I love my dad too, but my mom is really my best friend. We love to watch sports together. I love football, basketball, golf, soccer, tennis. I love it all."

Aaron said, "Did you play sports in school?"

Eva said, "I ran track and played volleyball and tennis."

Aaron asked, "Were you good?"

Eva laughed, "You want to race? Don't let this body fool you."

They both laughed. The more they talked, the more they laughed. Eva and Aaron ended up at dinner in a piano bar. They ate dinner and Aaron asked the piano player to let him play.

Eva heard the piano introduction to "A Song for You" then there was his voice. "I've been so many places in my life and times..."

Eva watched as Aaron sang the song. A tear rolled down her cheek. She felt so much joy inside her soul. This was a feeling she never had before. Her lips began to quiver. She wiped away her tears. Aaron finished the song with a piano solo and the audience gave him a standing ovation. When he finished the song, he got up and walked over to Eva. He whispered in her ear, "Eva, it doesn't matter whether it's two months, two years, or two decades, you are my something special. Let's explore us... together."

Chapter 7

After two days in Quebec City Eva and Aaron realized that they must spend some more time together. They had breakfast, lunch, and dinner together and had many conversations on life. On the last day in Quebec, Eva downloaded Tchaikovsky's Symphony No 6. She told Aaron to listen to the entire piece. During their last dinner Aaron said his next trip was to Sydney Australia. He was meeting a band there to perform for two nights.

Eva just stared at Aaron.

Aaron asked, "What, Eva?" He looked concerned. "What is it?"

Eva smiled. "I'm actually heading for the Blue Mountains in Australia."

Aaron said, "Now this is very interesting."

The next morning, Eva and Aaron checked in at the gate in the airport. They were assigned first class seats next to each other. During the plane ride they talked about their lives and their bucket lists.

Eva said, "There is one thing that I want to do very soon... I need to see my birth mother. She came to see me when I was in the hospital. She played my favorite song. Although I never met her, I feel connected to her. I really need to meet her before it's too late. She's 70 years old and very sick now."

"Wow. You are two decades apart too."

"You know what? You are right. Twenty years, two decades. just like you and me."

"No, we are 12 years apart."

"But still two decades." Eva smiled and continued her conversation with Aaron.

The flight to Sydney was exceptionally long, with a change of aircraft in Los Angeles. When they boarded the plane in Los Angeles Aaron asked Eva, "What was it like?"

"What was what like?"

"Heaven."

Eva looked out of the window at the clouds. "I remember everything was very bright and colorful. There was an overwhelming feeling of peace and serenity. I saw a man smiling at me. I didn't know him but he was familiar. I can't explain it, Aaron. I wanted to stay but he wouldn't let me. The doctors said I coded twice in the hospital, but I only remember the bright light once, and that was when I was in the car right after the accident. It was so peaceful. I also heard music. I remember thinking... they have violins in heaven."

"Who do you think the man was?"

"I don't know." Eva sat back and placed her chin on her hand. She closed her eyes and visualized the man. All of a sudden something inside her said, *It was your dad.* She opened her eyes and said, "It was my dad. My dad I never met. My dad died in a car crash in 1967." She realized when her mother showed her the pictures in the sunroom, one of them was the man she saw when she died. "I guess my dad knew it wasn't my time."

Eva and Aaron had a long conversation about divine purpose. Aaron asked, "Eva what do you think our divine purpose is?"

Eva said, "I think when you find work that you really love so much that it's like play, you are on your way to finding your divine purpose. If the work helps others, if the work teaches love, if the work spreads joy and peace… I remember when my best friend's sister died, I took her to a movie a few months later. It was a comedy. We laughed so hard that evening. Gina told me she hadn't laughed at all since her sister died. I found a venue where the comedian in the movie was performing a show. I got tickets for us and we laughed so much I almost peed my pants. That comedian changed Gina's life. She was no longer depressed and started to work again. I truly believe that comedian has found his divine purpose. To make people laugh. It's hard work to spread laughter and joy. He has sold-out audiences everywhere he goes."

Aaron said, "That's one way to think about it. I think life is all about finding love and ultimately finding love is your divine purpose, to spread love around the world. You, as a college professor and philosopher, help your students find truth and freedom. Not only that, they can define truth and freedom after they take your class. In my music, I write of truth and freedom. I learned at a young age not to let others define who I am. Many people I know still let others tell them what they can and cannot do. They are held back from living their best life because they don't know who they are. They are what someone else thinks they are. That's sad."

"My music is a microcosm of my experiences in life. I write about the polarization in our country and how different groups try to change the narrative in our country to make our nation a better place to live, while others try to keep people oppressed. My mother told me there was nothing that I couldn't do. She told me to dream big, have faith, and believe in myself. My mother taught me to never let anyone define who I am. She told me not to let anyone get in the way of my goals and dreams. Work hard for what you want and believe in yourself even if no one else does. My dad taught me how to set long- and short-term goals. He taught me how to manage money and showed me how to invest. Both of my parents molded me into the person I am."

"Although my parents were divorced both had a profound impact on my life. Both of my parents went to college and taught me that my education would set me free to do whatever I wanted to do.

Most ignorance in the world is because of lack of education. How can anyone think that the color of your skin makes you better than someone else? One day there will be a world where we all realize we are all brothers and sisters."

Eva listened to Aaron and was amazed at his wisdom. She looked in Aaron's eyes and smiled when he talked. The intellectual conversation was stimulating and refreshing for Eva.

Eva told Aaron about a professional development seminar she attended when she was a young graduate student. "I attended a class on gender equity and bias in education. For the warm-up activity the facilitator asked the adult students if they were born a different race or gender, how would their life be different. Aaron, you would be surprised at the responses. There was a man that said he could not even think of himself as a woman, so he would not go there. This was interesting, as he clearly had feminine mannerisms in the class, which he attributed to being raised around all women with no brothers or dad present. I'm not sure why he had to explain that to us. Anyway, he was a white male, and said if he was black, he would not be as successful as he is because blacks did not have the same privileges in the neighborhood he grew up in."

"For real?"

"Yes, Aaron. Another adult student, a black female said if she were born a male and white, she would be a doctor or a lawyer. Out of 20 students, I was the only one that said if I were a male and white, my life would not be different. I would be doing the same thing I am doing now. Being a different gender or race does not determine what you can or cannot do. I would never let my race or gender dictate my success in life. Everyone looked at me, while the facilitator smiled at me. She knew her work was cut out for her." Aaron said, "It's amazing how some people think that. I'm not being judgmental, but I've met plenty of poor people and rich people. The difference between their success was not the money they had or lack thereof. Some economically disadvantaged people I know had the drive and initiative to change the cycle of poverty in their family. In fact, one of the poorest kids in my high school was the valedictorian. She didn't let her circumstances define who she was. She didn't have a library in her home like we did. She studied at the library. They didn't have a car, but she took the bus to the library every weekend. I would always see her reading."

"One day I offered her a ride home. I could tell she was a little hesitant. When I dropped her off, she proudly said, 'This is where I live, but I won't live here forever. My parents work hard for what we have. One day, I am going to buy them a house in the country with lots of space for them to live out their senior years in comfort."

"That was 20 years ago. Today she owns her own insurance agency and has 100 people working for her. She takes care of her parents and bought them a house overlooking a golf course. What made her different from the other poor kids in her neighborhood? Her parents. They told her she could be whatever she wanted to be. Just believe in yourself and love God. Have faith, hope, and listen to your heart. She told everyone this during her graduation speech. She never forgot her old neighborhood. She was instrumental in creating a learning center around the corner from her old apartment where students could go for homework help. Now that, my friend, is an altruistic woman. The epitome of class."

"What a great story, Aaron. It's too bad the world doesn't see people like her. She should write a book and tell her story."

Eva and Aaron stopped talking for a moment.

"Look at the clouds, Aaron. They are lovely. I love to walk and take in the nature all around me."

Aaron said, "What was the most peaceful, serene moment of your life?"

"One night when I was in Cancun I looked into the sky from my balcony. I saw a star shining so bright. The next morning the paper said Venus was out last night. It was so peaceful watching the stars and Venus. That was nice. I also watched the sun come up one morning in Atlanta. I went to college downtown and had a condo on Peachtree Street. I used to stay up all night dancing with my friends on the weekend. One Sunday morning I was playing 'On the Wings of Love' on my record player."

"Record player?"

"Yes Aaron, they were still making albums then." She laughed. "Anyway, I looked outside and realized when the sun is rising it doesn't happen all at once. One side of the street was dark and it gradually got light. I never watched the sun rise before. It was so beautiful. I cried."

"So you haven't seen sunrise on the ocean?"

"No, but I've seen it rise on the lake behind my house."

"Well now, I'll have to take you to Hilton Head, SC to the Atlantic Ocean and let you watch the sunrise."

Eva asked Aaron, "What was the most peaceful, serene moment in your life?"

Aaron answered, "Watching you listen to me play the piano in Quebec City."

Eva said, "C'est si gentil."

Aaron said, "Je tombe amoureux."

A couple across the aisle looked at Eva and Aaron. "You two make a nice couple."

Chapter 8

Eva arrived at her chalet in the Blue Mountains. It was snowing when she arrived. She remembered it was winter in Australia in August. She walked onto her deck and saw the Blue Mountains and remembered the story of the three sisters from her previous visit. The Blue Mountains were just as famous as our Grand Canyon in the United States. The eucalyptus trees gave the blue mist throughout the mountain. It was absolutely beautiful. Eva planned to create a peaceful, serene atmosphere to enjoy the company of her new friend Aaron Kelly.

Aaron called his mother to tell him about the amazing woman he met in Quebec City. He told his mother he met the most amazing woman. "Mom, I met my soul mate in Quebec City. She is a professor and loves music and sports. She lives outside of Seattle, Washington. We have so much in common. Both of us almost died… she was in a car accident. That's another story, Mom. She is incredibly special.

I'll send you a picture of us when I get to the Blue Mountains. After this trip, I'm going to take off a few months and travel with her. She doesn't know it, but I think I'm going to spend the rest of my life with her. Mom, she was born on March 2, one day before me."

Aaron's mom said, "In 1980?"

"No Mom, in 1968. We are twelve years apart, but that doesn't matter. I really believe everyone has a soul mate and she is mine."

Aaron's mom said, "Aaron Chase Kelly!" Aaron knew he was in trouble when his mom said his full name. "Twelve years is a big difference. Does she have kids?"

"No. She's never been married."

"Aaron, I'm 60. She's only ten years younger than me."

"Mom!!!! You are not Eva."

"But I want grandchildren!"

"Well, maybe we will adopt some. By the way, 50-year-old women are having babies now and 50 is not old."

"Oh wow, Aaron. She's got you hooked. Does she know about your financial status?" "No Mom. We haven't talked about our assets but I can tell you she has her own money. She lives a life of privilege. I'll send a picture to you." Aaron sent a picture from his phone.

"Okay! Aaron, that woman is not 50. She looks 33!"

"Mom, she is 50. You will love her. I have to go. Love you. Hey, tell Dad I found my wife."

Mrs. Kelly got off the phone and called her ex-husband immediately. "Roger!"

"Hi! What's up, honey?"

"Aaron is in love with a woman 50 years old."

"Atta boy, Aaron!"

"What?"

"Well, you were two years older than me, Julia. What does she do for a living?"

"She's a college professor."

"That's right; I told my son to marry smart."

"Roger!!" Julia was concerned that Eva was too old for Aaron. Her ex-husband was thrilled.

"Julia, we raised Aaron to make good decisions in his life. If he loves, what's her name? Eva, let him love her."

"But what about our grandkids?"

"Julia... It's his life... let him figure it out. He can adopt or maybe she can have one or two."

"That's exactly what he said. Bye Roger."

"Bye Julia." As soon as Roger Kelly hung up he called Aaron to congratulate him. "I can't wait to meet her."

Chapter 9

Eva went to a local market to get fresh fruit and vegetables. She remembered Maria told her to eat right, take her meds, and exercise to keep her diabetes in check. When she was in the market a little lady with silver hair, a mole on her chin, and light green eyes told her that she was very special. The lady grabbed her hand and said that she would have a baby girl soon. Eva thought the lady was crazy because she was 50 years old and was not thinking of having a child. The lady also told her that she would live to be 100. The psychic told Eva that she would live in a mansion one day near a lake and a forest with lots of trees. She told her that she would help someone through a difficult time and save the lives of many people. "You have a gift. It's your voice. Continue to use your voice to help others."

As the lady walked away Eva said, "Will I find true love?"

The psychic said, "You already have." She smiled and walked away.

Eva thought about everything the psychic said. *I can't have a baby. What is wrong with her?* Eva said, "Hey wait a minute. Can you take a picture with me?"

"Sure!" The lady smiled as Eva took a selfie with the psychic. "Thank you! God bless you!" The lady smiled and walked away.

"Wait!" cried Eva. "What's your name?"

"Nicolette." Nicolette walked across the street and into another store.

"What an amazing experience."

Eva walked back to the house, smiling. "Umm, if I live to be 100, Aaron will be 88. That gives us at least 50 years together. Maybe the twelve years' age difference doesn't matter."

As she walked in the house she turned on classical music. She made a pot of tea while she waited for Aaron to arrive. She found a quiet place to meditate after her tea.

Aaron stopped at the same market to get some flowers for Eva. The psychic watched as Aaron crossed the street. She smiled.

Aaron knocked on the door and Eva welcomed him with open arms and showed him his bedroom. Eva gave him a tour around the house. She had a piano delivered just in case he wanted to play. That first evening, they laughed, told stories, and cooked together in the kitchen. Eva cooked the vegetables and Aaron cooked the salmon. They sat on the deck and ate their dinner. Aaron recommended they have a battle.

Eva said, "What kind of battle do you want to have with me?"

Aaron said, "A musical battle. Now get your classical music on your phone. Now I have mine."

Aaron played "If You Love Me" by Brownstone; Eva played Symphony No. 6, The Pathetique by Tchaikovsky. Aaron played "Can't get Enough of Your Love" by Barry White; Eva played Beethoven's Moonlight Sonata. Aaron played "Here and Now" by Luther Vandross' Eva played Canon in D by Pachelbel.

Aaron said, "Wait a minute, isn't that a wedding song?"

"Isn't 'Here and Now' a wedding song?" They both laughed.

Aaron sighed, "You know, I'm a little tired."

"Well, go to bed. Get some rest. I need to call my mom."

Aaron thanked Eva for dinner. He smiled and walked into his bedroom.

Eva walked over and placed her phone on a speaker and turned on Kenny G's "Forever Love."

Aaron turned his head and said, "What do you know about Kenny G?"

"I live in Seattle." Eva laughed again. Eva called her mom and told her about her young new friend. Her mother was happy for her.

An hour later Aaron came out of his room in his pajamas while Eva was journaling. "What's wrong, Aaron? Can't sleep?"

"No, I can't. I'm just so excited to be here and to get to know you better."

Eva looked at Aaron and said, "You had a long day. Come here."

Aaron walked over to Eva, who was sitting on a couch near the fireplace. He lay down and placed his head on her lap. He turned over on his side. Eva stroked his hair and began to sing to "Annie's Song" by John Denver.

As Eva sang the song Aaron was thinking, *Oh my goodness. She can sing. This truly is my soul mate.* Aaron fell asleep.

Chapter 10

When Aaron woke up, he was in his bed. He did not know how he got there. He wiped his eyes and followed the sound of the classical music to the deck. There was Eva in a white gown sipping tea and listening to her song. When Aaron arrived, they looked at each other but did not speak. They were speaking with their eyes. It was snowing and Eva shivered a little. Aaron saw her robe on the chair and covered her shoulders and kissed them. Eva poured Aaron some tea. Aaron watched every move Eva made. Finally, he walked over to her held her hand and led her back in the house. He put on "A Year Ago" by Kenny G. He lay down with Eva on a white rug that was on the floor. Her long black hair and her brown skin were the only color on the rug. He said, "Eva, I think I'm in love."

Eva said, "Aaron, what is love?"

Aaron said, "Love is waking up having tea in the Blue Mountains with you. Love is sharing an airplane ride with a beautiful lady who died, went to heaven, and came back … for me. Love is playing the piano in front of a crowd, knowing there is one lady there who has my heart. Love is staring me right in the eyes, looking at me right now. Eva, you are my everything. Let's explore this world together and perhaps together, we can find our divine purpose."

Eva remembered the psychic who said she had found her true love. Eva told Aaron, "I know I'm in love with you. Aaron, I love you." Eva laid her head on Aaron's shoulder as he kissed her hair. They embraced each other tightly for several minutes. After the embrace, they looked into each other's eyes and kissed.

Chapter 11

Eva flew back to Seattle and Aaron flew back to Las Vegas. Eva was thrilled to tell her best friend Gina Newton about her newfound love. Gina called Eva to meet her at her new house that evening. Eva had never been there so she had to get the directions.

As soon as she got in her car her rear light indicator came on in her Mercedes. While Eva was driving a police officer pulled her over. "Oh boy! Here we go!" Eva turned on her web cam. The police are supposed to protect and serve; however, in recent news there has been a lot of excessive force, police brutality, and murder involving the police.

Eva rolled her window down and kept on her dark shades as the officer walked over to the right side of her car. She wondered why he walked over to the passenger side and not the driver side. He asked for her license and registration. The officer proceeded to tell Eva she was driving 45 in a 30-mph zone.

"I've never been on this road before, officer. I didn't know the speed limit."

"Another reason for you to slow down. Also, you have a light out."

"That light just came on when I got in my car today."

The police officer laughed and said, "That's what they all say."

Eva noticed the police officer was kind of friendly. He gave her back her license and registration and said, "Slow down and get that light fixed."

"You know I'm recording you. Is that why you are being so nice?"

The officer lifted his head in the air and said, "All cops are not bad cops. Most of us do a really good job of serving and protecting. The ones that don't give all of us a bad name. My department provided sensitivity training to all our officers. There is also a new class in basic training on treating people as people, not objects. Now, you said you were never on this road before. Where are you going?"

"I'm going to meet my friend at her new home on Lakeview Estates Street."

"Oh that's my parent's neighborhood. Just take a left at the light and turn right on Avalon. You will be right there in five minutes."

Eva took off her shades and thanked the officer for the directions and shook his hand. "Dr. O'Sullivan?" The officer was surprised to see that the woman driving the car was his old Counseling Theory and Practice college professor. "Dr. O'Sullivan! Hi!" The officer covered his mouth with his right hand and his eyes were wide open. "You were the best teacher I ever had throughout all my education. Dr. O'Sullivan, I use some of the things you taught us in my job every day. Wow. It's so good to see you again."

Eva gave the officer her card and said, "Call me. I want to hear more about the work the police officers are doing with sensitivity training. Maybe I can help too. Good to see you... Shawn? Right?"

Officer Shawn Gates smiled as Eva pulled away.

When Eva arrived at Gina Newton's house she told her about the encounter with Officer Gates. "Gina, I just spent the best eight weeks of my life with a wonderful man. We kept running into each other, everywhere. There is an old saying that everyone has a soul mate. I think Aaron is mine."

"Eva, you just met him. How do you know?"

"I just know," Eva said. "We have so much in common. We like the same things. When he looks at me I feel warm inside. I... I... It's like that Nikki Giovanni poem 'Resignation.' I am just resigned to love him."

"How old is he and what does he do for a living?"

"He is a musician and he is 38 years old."

"THIRTY-EIGHT!! You are 12 years older than he is! Girl... Does he know you are wealthy? Is he looking for a sugar mamma?"

"Stop. Stop. No Gina. We haven't talked about our financial status, but I can tell he takes care of himself. He is a self-made man who's traveling the world just like me looking for his purpose. His parents are divorced but still friends, and he is highly intelligent. He speaks French too. We are both bilingual, but I think he's trilingual."

"Eva, I don't know honey. What if you get married and he wants kids?"

"Gina! A little old lady in Australia told me that I was going to have a child and I already found true love."

"Now I need a drink! Eva, you have eggs." Gina was laughing and chuckling. Eva took a long look at Gina. "Eva, you are 12 years older than—what's his name?"

"Gina, she also said I was going to live to be 100! If I do marry Aaron, he will be 88 when I die. We can spend 50 years together." She had been sipping on wine and was almost finished with the bottle.

"Well, Eva, if it's meant to be… it will happen. But a baby, Eva?? I just don't know about that."

They both laughed and Gina sipped wine while Eva sipped tea. Suddenly Eva told Gina something that she did not know. "Gina… I froze my eggs when I was 35. I have eggs." Gina dropped her glass. "I can have them unfrozen and fertilized."

Eva wondered if her eggs were still good. She knew that all eggs didn't survive the thaw.

Chapter 12

Aaron arrived back home in Las Vegas and met with his friend Rondell Rogers. Rondell was 38 years old, very tall and handsome. When Aaron and Rondell walked in a room people automatically thought they were professional athletes. They went to college together at Florida A & M. Both pledged Omega Psi Phi. They always wore royal purple and gold. They both liked nice cars. Aaron drove a Bentley and Rondell drove a Maybach.

No one knew the story behind the wealth of these two men except their close friends. When they were in college they bought a lotto ticket and won $550 million dollars. The two split the winnings after taxes and invested well. Rondell received his Master's degree in Business Administration with a minor in Art History and was also Aaron's financial advisor. Aaron majored in music and minored in French in college. They learned how to golf in high school and played in college. Although they won a lot of money, they still finished school and worked while traveling the world. They had the best of everything but did not let their wealth define who they were.

Once at a casino pool party a couple of girls walked over to them to ask them what team they played for. They smiled and said, "No, we are musicians."

The girls laughed and said, "No. We know you are football players."

Aaron thought, *Some people always stereotype tall black males driving nice cars as professional athletes.*

The girls saw them get out of their cars and walk into the hotel lobby. Aaron's friend was DJ'ing a pool party and invited them to come. They were in a VIP booth when they saw the two ladies again. The ladies continued to try to figure out what team they played for. Finally, one of the girls noticed a horseshoe on their shoulders. "The Colts!" The girls shouted, "You play for the Colts."

Aaron and Rondell looked at each other and laughed hysterically. "No ladies. We are Q's."

"Q's? What's that?" The ladies walked away looking confused.

Aaron said, "I am so glad I don't have to deal with this kind of stuff anymore. I met the lady of my dreams. She is smart, beautiful, spiritual, and she loves me unconditionally." "Congrats, man!" Rondell said. "Who is this lady? Where is she from? How old is she?"

"Her name is Eva Whitfield O'Sullivan."

"Dude, you have an Irish woman?"

"Non elle n'est pas."

"Noir de shes?"

"Oui homme, elle est noire." After they finished a little conversation in French Aaron answered the rest of the questions. "She is adopted and is from Seattle, WA. She was born in Columbia, SC. Her father died before she was born and her mother gave her up for adoption. She's never met her birth mother, who is a retired judge. She lives on a plantation in Salters, SC. Eva is 50 years old but brother, she doesn't look like it. I love her, man. She is amazing. Rondell, she loves classical music... Tchaikovsky... She is very sweet, Rondell. She's going to be the mother of my children."

"Aaron, she's 50!!"

"Well, she can still have kids or we can adopt. We can get an egg donor." Aaron did not know that Eva stored her eggs when she was 35 years old.

Rondell was happy for Aaron but felt it was too soon to be planning for babies. "Hey man, let's go to the art studio. You have inspired me to create a painting: Two Decades Apart."

Chapter 13

It was another rainy day in Seattle, Washington when Eva went to Gina's school to facilitate a group session with some students who were having problems with he said, she said. The group had several mediations but nothing worked. Eva was fingerprinted and volunteered a lot in the local schools. Eva was a motivational speaker and had written several self-help books. When Eva walked into the school, she had to give security her ID to be scanned in a machine. This was a safeguard for the school to keep out predators. Next she was given a visitors' badge and escorted to the group counseling session.

There were nine girls in the session, a professional school counselor, a peer mediator, and Gina, the principal. Eva was facilitating the meeting so she stated the objective of the group (what is the real issue of the feud) and made some ground rules. "Let all voices be heard. Be honest and open. Be an active participant. Listen while others speak. Speak directly to individuals. Don't blame or judge others. Ask for clarification if needed. Put all cellular devices away and off. Everything remains in the group and confidential." Eva also said if anyone said anything regarding hurting themselves or someone else, it must be reported. She asked the group if anyone wanted to add to the norms. One of the students said, "Be respectful at all times."

Everyone shared their name and grade level. Eva shared information about herself and then asked the group what they expected to get from the group. The group agreed that they needed to learn how to handle adversity without fighting and bullying on social media. They also wanted to learn who their real friends were. Too much he said, she said had led to fights and broken friendships.

Gina gave Eva some background information on the group. Over the summer there were several altercations in the neighborhood that trickled into school during the beginning of the year. It all began when Ariel received a message from Cassie on Twitter that her boyfriend Craig was seen with another girl at the movie. Ariel did not believe it so Cassie took a picture and sent it to Ariel on Messenger. Ariel was fuming and called her other friends to tell them what Cassie said. That night Craig called Ariel to tell her goodnight and to his surprise, Ariel did not want to talk to him. He could not figure out why Ariel was angry with him. The next day some of Cassie's friends told Craig that Cassie sent Ariel a picture on Messenger showing him with another girl. Craig said that was his cousin visiting from Canada and she invited him out with her boyfriend, who was also there but had gone to the concession stand when Craig hugged his cousin and said he was glad to see her. Craig also said he sent Ariel a message the day before asking her if she wanted to go but received no response. Evidently Ariel did not get the message. When Ariel found out the truth, she went to fight Cassie, but her crew was there waiting to defend her. As a result, Ariel got her crew and planned a group fight at the park near their home. No one was thinking about the consequences. Some of Ariel's friends were 18 and could have been arrested for assault. The fight happened and the police were called but they all ran before anyone got hurt. Now, both girls were using social media to harass and bully each other.

Eva used the Rational Emotive Therapy (RET) approach to work with the students. Eva worked on Ariel first as the group listened. "I'm going to teach you about the ABC's. A is the activating event. B is how that made you feel. C is your reaction. All of you take a minute and write down your ABCs of this event." After three minutes Eva worked on Ariel first.

"A – What was the activating event, Ariel?"

"Cassie lying about my boyfriend."

"B – How did that make you feel?"

"Angry and very upset!"

"C – So what did you do?"

"I confronted her about the lie and wanted to beat her ass."

A student said, "Let's make another rule and refrain from foul language." Everyone agreed.

"D – What could you have done differently?"

Ariel was quiet. Someone tried to talk but Eva said, "Let her think about it. Given the fact that it was actually Craig's cousin on a date with her boyfriend and he also invited you to go the day before, do you think your actions were rational or irrational, Ariel?"

Ariel was still silent but Eva could see she was thinking and listening. Eva had a way of knowing what people felt. She smiled at Ariel and said, "I'll come back to you."

Eva asked the group to respond individually. Most said they should have gotten all the facts before they made an assumption about Craig. Ariel's crew said they could have been more supportive by telling her to communicate with Craig before she shut him out.

No one was dealing with the fact that Ariel fought Cassie.

Finally, one student spoke up. "Cassie knew that was Craig's cousin." Everyone was quiet. This was the first time everyone heard this.

One of Cassie's friends said, "If I'm being honest… I heard that too."

Eva looked for Ariel's response. She was surprised Ariel was so calm. Instead of getting angry Ariel asked Cassie, "Is this true?" Cassie said yes. "Why Cassie?"

Cassie told Ariel she was mad with Craig because she heard that Craig told her friend that she was a piece of trash. Eva said, "Who told you that?"

Cassie pointed to one of her friends. "I didn't say it. I heard it from someone else."

Eva said, "And you repeated what you heard and not what you knew was a fact?" Once again everyone was silent.

Suddenly Crystal, one of Ariel's friends, said, "He didn't say that. I told you to leave him alone because that was my friend's boyfriend. Craig told Scotty that you tried to come onto him and he turned you down flat. This is what I know because I saw it, Cassie. Behind the gym... last week after volleyball practice. Craig did not say you are a piece of trash. He said you are a piece of work, trying to come on to your friend's boyfriend."

Gina was amazed at the progress that was being made but wondered how she was going to get Ariel not to hate Cassie after all of this. Cassie began to cry and apologize. Ariel went over to Cassie and accepted her apology but told her that her actions could have gotten them all locked up or suspended. She just had one question. "Why my boyfriend?" Eva was watching Ariel and her intuition kicked in. "Ariel, come back to your seat." Eva watched Ariel closely. She saw something no one else saw.

Another student said, "Maybe we should make that a norm."

"Group, let's take a 20-minute snack break." Gina ordered lunch for the group. Students like to eat.

Eva told Gina to put on Symphony No. 6 until she returned. There was one silent member in the group that Eva watched closely. It was obvious she had something going on and she appeared troubled. Eva told Ariel and Cassie to come with her. They met in the principal's office with a school counselor present. She went through the ABC's with them individually and then together. Eva realized that Ariel was covering up her feelings and she wanted Ariel to know that people make mistakes in life. If you learn the lesson from the mistakes, it becomes a positive experience. Eva requested to speak to the parents of both students. Both parents agreed to the group counseling session. Without going into the specifics of what happened during the group sessions, the students were able to talk to their parents about the resolution. The two girls were not friends afterwards but they were respectful to each other and never used social media again to hurt each other. Cassie continued to meet with her school counselor as she had several self-esteem issues she needed to resolve.

Eva also told Gina to keep an eye on a group member named Diamond. She believed that Diamond might be struggling with something. Diamond reminded Eva of an abused student that was in her class once and she had to call social services to assist. Gina agreed to follow up with Diamond. "Students have so many things to worry about these days. School is no longer a safe place like it used to be. The violence, bullying, and use of social media to harass others is at an all-time high. It doesn't start in school. It starts in the neighborhood and trickles into school. It's a tough job having to handle discipline and make instruction our main priority. It's hard. We can't get to instruction because kids are fighting all the time over he said, she said. Every day when I go home, I'm exhausted. I'm glad I have you to talk to, Eva. For some reason, you understand and you get it. Many people don't. They think it's the school, but it's not. It's the community that needs to come together to discuss what's in the best interest of these students. I'm going to have a community forum soon. I'll invite you to come. Perhaps if we can get peace in the neighborhood, we can have peace in schools."

"Yes, Gina. You are right. It takes a village. I've noticed most of the parents that I talk to are young parents. They need support too. A lot of them had bad experiences in school and some dropped out because they had children. We also have a lot of parents with college degrees. The level of education doesn't matter in some cases. Some students rebel at a certain age and don't want to listen to the adults. They'd rather listen to their friends. We should survey our parents to determine what kind of support they need from the school and community. We just cannot assume what their needs are. Just let me know. I'll be willing to assist in any way I can. Love you, Gina."

Gina watched as Eva walked to her car. "Now that is an amazing person. There is no one like Eva Whitfield O'Sullivan."

When Eva left, Gina called Diamond on the phone and told her to meet her in the office in the morning. The next morning Diamond showed up and appeared sad and tired. Gina asked Diamond, "What's wrong, Diamond?"

"I've been awake all night and I threw up this morning," Diamond said.

"Are you pregnant, Diamond?"

"I don't know."

"Perhaps you need to go to the doctor. There is a free clinic around the corner. If you are, you have to take care of yourself and get prenatal care. Does your mother know?"

"No. But how did you know there was something wrong?"

"You know... Dr. O'Sullivan told me to keep an eye on you. She's so intuitive and insightful."

"Well, I know I'm pregnant. I took a pregnancy test. I haven't told my mom, but I will. My boyfriend moved last week to Connecticut. I told him, but he doesn't want to have anything to do with me or the baby. I'm keeping it, though. I just don't know how I'm going to make it through school."

"Don't you worry about that. I will make sure you stay in school and graduate on time. You just have to continue to do the work and make plans. You will have lots of support."

Gina embraced Diamond as she cried about the situation. While she was in the principal's office, Diamond called her mom and told her about the pregnancy. Fortunately, Diamond's mother understood what she was going through, as she had her first child at 15 with an abandoned boyfriend. She assured Diamond that it wasn't the end of the world, and that she would help her through this.

Gina said, "Can I share your situation with Dr. O'Sullivan? She is really concerned about you."

"Yes. There is something about that lady that I admire. You can tell her, but no one else."

When Diamond left school to go to the doctor, Gina called Eva and told her the news.

Eva was not surprised and for some reason, she had collected a lot of books on childbirth. After her conversation with Nicolette, she started watching babies' births on the Discovery Channel and YouTube videos. Eva was slowly becoming an expert on childbirth and didn't really know why. Eva told Gina to keep her posted on Diamond and make sure that she stayed in school. She also told Gina if Diamond needed a partner for birthing classes, she would be there.

After her talk with Gina, she called Aaron to see when he was coming to Seattle. She told him about her work with her friend's high school and how she introduced a group of students to Tchaikovsky. She also told Aaron about the possibility of working with the parents of some students. Aaron said that was a great idea and to let him know if he could assist in any way. She did not tell him about Diamond's situation.

"Eva, I can't wait to get to Seattle. I'll be there in a few months."

"Bring an umbrella, Aaron. It rains every day." They both laughed.

Chapter 14

It had been four months since Eva and Aaron met. They talked on the phone every day and learned more things about each other as the days passed. Eva had Maria pick up Aaron from the airport. When Maria saw Aaron, she said to herself, *She has found herself a god.*

"You must be Maria! I heard so much about you."

"And I have heard so much about you, Mr. Kelly."

"No, call me Aaron." They drove up to the house on the lake and Aaron looked around at the beauty of the property. "Eva has great taste in houses."

Maria said, "Eva has great taste in everything." She smiled and showed Aaron his room. Eva shared everything with Maria and so she knew they had not had a physical relationship. All the love was based solely on inner feeling and pure thoughts. Aaron walked around the house before Eva arrived from her university. He walked on the deck overlooking the lake. Maria brought him some tea exactly like he liked it. Aaron asked Maria to sit down.

Maria said, "Eva drinks her tea here every morning."

"Yes. I know we both have similar routines."

"You know, you have made her very happy. Thank you for finding her. After her accident, we didn't know if she'd be the same. Eva is even better than before. It's like she has been enlightened. She has a lot of conventional wisdom and funded knowledge, but she just knows so much about life and the world. I love listening to her talk. Her philosophies on education, politics, and even death are inspirational and enlightening."

As soon as Maria finished her sentence, Eva walked through the door in a black dress with white pearls and white trim at the bottom. She had a black raincoat and umbrella that Maria took from her at the door. She could hardly get out of her coat before Aaron rushed to her side and embraced her. Maria watched and walked over to the wall and turned on Tchaikovsky.

"Welcome home, sweetheart," Eva said.

Aaron told Eva he loved her house. "What did you do, write a couple of million-seller books?"

Eva smiled. "Let's sit down. My birth mother inherited millions of dollars from my grandfather after he passed. The inheritance was more than anyone knew. The grantor is my grandfather, who established the trust when he got ill. He wrote in his will the beneficiaries were my birth mother, his only child, and her firstborn (me). The Trustees are my adoptive parents. They have done a great job managing my assets and trust. Mom was a stay-at-home mom but she had a Master's degree in Business Management."

"So does my best friend Rondell, from FAMU."

"I've seen pictures of your house and car; you must have a trust somewhere," Eva said. Aaron looked at Eva. "Nope. It's a long story. I'll tell you later."

Eva and Aaron spent the evening talking and sharing stories. Eva took a break from storytelling to take a walk in the rain with Aaron. Aaron could not believe that Eva thought walking in the rain would be fun. It actually was fun for Aaron and exercise for Eva. She had to continue to eat right, and exercise because diabetes and heart disease ran in her family. When they returned from the walk Eva received a phone call from her mom saying her birth mother had to go on dialysis. Eva knew she needed to meet her soon. She just had a feeling inside that her birth mom wouldn't be here long.

Chapter 15

Maria cooked dinner for Eva and Aaron and her parents the next day. The O'Sullivans loved Aaron. They could tell he was an educated man and that he really loved their daughter. Colonel O'Sullivan invited Aaron outside on the front porch to smoke a cigar. Aaron said politely, "I don't smoke."

Colonel O'Sullivan began to tell war stories about Vietnam. He talked about his days in Fort Jackson, SC. Aaron told Colonel O'Sullivan that his mom and dad grew up in Columbia, SC and his dad sold real estate there. "He's retired now and moved to Hilton Head, SC."

As the colonel continued to talk, he said he liked to golf in Hilton Head and used to go every summer. "Last summer we took a side trip to Charleston. My wife's family is from there. She went to visit her family and I went fishing with a group of old Army officers. I met this fellow named Anthony Shaw from Charleston."

Aaron cut him off, "Anthony Shaw? Do they call him Shorty?"

"Yeah, we called him Shorty. He was about five feet four but he always said he was five ten." They both laughed.

"Colonel, that's my dad's old fishing buddy! It's such a small world."

The colonel called his wife, "Helen, come out here. Aaron knows Shorty."

The rest of the evening the men told Shorty stories while Eva caught her mom up on all her adventures with Aaron. "Mom, I think I'm going to tell him about the eggs."

"Is it that serious?"

"Yes. He's the one."

Chapter 16

Aaron stayed a week in Seattle, and Eva decided to fly back to Las Vegas with him. When they arrived at the airport Rondell picked them up. Rondell was in awe of Eva's beauty and grace. When she walked out of baggage claim Rondell grabbed her bag and said, "Hello, Mrs. Kelly!" Eva liked the way that sounded. The airport was close to the Vegas strip and Eva told Aaron she was Lady Luck and wanted to go play blackjack before they left. Aaron already made plans for Eva, and Eva made plans for Aaron.

One night Aaron was playing in a piano bar in a casino. Rondell was there with Eva while the jazz band played. All of a sudden one of the band members whispered something to the guitar player and the drummer. Aaron nodded. The guitar player said, "We have a special request from the audience."

At that time Eva walked to the stage, looking like a million dollars. The band began to play "Always be my baby." Eva began to sing the song. Aaron's eyes were so big. He looked at Rondell. Rondell nodded his head. "We were as one, babe, for a moment in time…" Eva sang. She turned to Aaron and sang directly to him. Aaron cried. Tears rolled down his cheeks as he played the piano.

Rondell had his hands on his head like he just could not believe what was happening. "You should just go to the Elvis chapel and get married."

Eva sat down and Aaron had a little piano solo. Eva realized that it was "Here and now." He looked at Eva while he sang. Eva cried. After the show Aaron said, "Eva, you've been holding out on me. You can sing??"

"I sang for you in the Blue Mountains."

"Not like that. Let's go home."

When Eva arrived back at Aaron's house she kissed him in the doorway. As she looked around she said, "Do all musicians live like this?"

Aaron said, "Okay, I'll tell you later. The true story. First, I have something important I want to do."

"Aaron, first I want to tell you something."

"No, let me tell you first." Aaron went to the piano in his home and played and sang "Thinking Out Loud."

As Aaron sang, Eva cried. Rondell came in with Eva's parents, Aaron's parents, Gina, and of course, little Shorty. After Aaron finished the song he got down on one knee and pulled out a blue box with a Tiffany and Co. platinum five-carat diamond ring. "Eva, will you marry me?"

Eva said, "Yes."

As soon as Eva said yes, Rondell pulled the curtain that overlooked the mountains and a full orchestra was on the deck playing Symphony No. 6, the Pathetique.

Eva was so surprised. She looked around and saw Maria was there too. Aaron had chartered two planes to get the families together. Eva was so happy. She was finally engaged to the man of her dreams. Everyone was happy and celebrating.

Aaron took Eva by the hand and went into a room in his house that was quiet. He showed her a picture that was 15 years old. "I won the lottery when I was 23 years old. In fact, Rondell and I won together. Two college students. Sometimes I think about how I almost died as a child and I lived to win $250 million dollars."

"What?"

"After taxes!"

"Oh me."

"So you see, Eva, I can take care of you. You can work if you'd like but we can take off and travel the world together. Let's live our life."

"You know, a psychic in Australia told me that I would live to be 100. That means we have over 50 possible years together."

"That is if I live to be 100 also."

"She also said that I was going to have a child."

"Let's talk about this. We can adopt kids."

Eva smiled. "Nope, we can have our own baby. I froze my eggs."

"What? Let's go! Okay, let's get Gina to carry them."

"Aaron, when I was in college my roommate was a girl named Samantha. Anyway, Samantha married a guy from college when she was 21 and had a child they named Lisa. It didn't work out. She divorced her husband and has been dating the same woman for 12 years, Professor Angel Baptiste. She's also a professor at my school. I introduced them. Anyway, her daughter Lisa is 28 years old and single. One day we all had lunch together and her mom was telling how grateful she was for me introducing her to Angel. She said she could never repay me. Samantha asked me when I was going to thaw my eggs out. Lisa said, 'What eggs?' I told her if I wasn't married or in a relationship after I was 35, I'd have my eggs frozen. I think they are still good. It's been 15 years. By the way, I still can have a child, if you know what I mean. Anyway, Lisa said she would carry my child if I ever wanted a baby. I'd just have to find a donor. Well, you know what, sweetheart, after we are married we can try the old-fashioned way. If it doesn't work, we have options. I love you. I know there are risks having a baby after a certain age but whatever God wills."

Aaron looked at Eva and touched her stomach. "One way or another, it will happen. My mother will be happy to have a grandchild."

When Eva and Aaron returned to the room, love, happiness, and peace filled the room.

Chapter 17

That night Eva was happy but for some reason she could not sleep. Every time she was about to fall to sleep, she started to dream. Eva dreamt a lot but could never remember her dreams. On this night, Eva remembered everything in her dream. She was back in Sydney, Australia with Nicolette. Nicolette invited Eva to her house to show her some paintings her mother drew. Eva loved art and was impressed by the art collection Nicolette had in her home. Nicolette never said where she was from but told Eva she had an older sister and a brother who died years ago. Nicolette spoke about growing up in a beautiful city full of museums and rich in history. Nicolette was also a tea drinker and shared a pot of tea with Eva on her porch. Eva told Nicolette about her birth mother and her adoptive parents. Nicolette told Eva in her dream that she needed to go see her mother. Her time on earth was almost gone. She would have eternal life in another realm but her mother wanted to see her before she left this earth.

Eva woke up and looked at Aaron sleeping soundly next to her. She called her mother to check on Daisy. Ms. O'Sullivan told Eva that her mother was stable but on dialysis three times a week.

"I have to go see her." Eva did not tell her mom about the dream but she did tell Aaron. When Aaron woke up Eva had cooked him breakfast and brought it to him on a tray. They blessed the food and ate together in the bed. Eva fed Aaron fresh strawberries and cream and Aaron fed Eva fresh cantaloupe with blueberries. "Aaron, I love you so much. I can't even imagine my life without you."

"Well, you will never have to worry about that. I'm yours. Are you ready to play some blackjack today, Lady Luck?"

"Well now! What do you think? Let's go!!"

Chapter 18

Eva and Aaron decided they wanted to go to a casino and play blackjack. This was Eva's first day out wearing her engagement ring. She kept looking at it and smiling. *I've got to plan a wedding!* Eva told Aaron, "You know they call me Lady Luck."

"I bet they do. I'm the lucky one. I have you."

"Okay Aaron, do you know how to play blackjack? Don't mess up the cards now!" Eva had a smile on her face as Aaron looked at her with a smile.

"Of course I know how to play. I live in Vegas, baby." They sat down at the blackjack table with Rondell looking on.

The dealer dealt Eva an Ace for her first card, and Aaron had a Nine of Hearts. The dealer had a six showing. Eva's next card was a Queen of Hearts. Eva's firsthand was blackjack. "Wow Eva! You are lucky."

Aaron's next card was a six of clubs. "Hit me!"

"No Aaron, the dealer has a 6 showing. You have to stay!" Eva looked confused.

Aaron laughed, "No, I was just kidding! I'm staying."

The dealer turned over his card. The dealer had a 16 and busted on the Ten of Clubs. Eva went on to win every hand she played, while Aaron lost half of his chips.

"I feel real lucky. I'm going to play the max. If I win, let's go. If I lose, it was fun." The dealer dealt Eva another Ace of Spades.

Aaron had an Ace, too. "I should have gone all in too." They both laughed.

Eva had blackjack and so did Aaron. They both looked at each other and said, "Let's go." They cashed in their chips and went with Rondell to the lobby bar to listen to a local band.

"You are pretty lucky Eva. You did not lose one hand. That's unheard of."

Eva just raised her eyebrows a little and shook her head from side to side. "I practice online. It's just a fun thing to do. I'm thirsty; let's get something to drink."

Rondell told a story about being in Florida and hitting a jackpot at the Hard Rock Café Hotel and Casino. He never hit a jackpot before but he said it was a lot of fun.

"How would you like to go to the Grand Canyon tomorrow, Eva? Have you ever been there?"

"No, I haven't, but I'm not in the mood for a long ride."

"Oh no. We would fly there by helicopter."

"That sounds like a great idea, man. I can get some nice photos." Rondell was an amateur photographer and had a collection of pictures and art from all the places he has visited. "Okay! Next trip, Grand Canyon!"

Eva went back to Aaron's house and packed her bags. In the meantime, she told all her friends she was engaged to Aaron and was ready to start planning her wedding. Her family and friends who were at the engagement party left on the same day. They had brunch together that morning with Eva and Aaron. Everyone was excited about blending the families and the future of Eva and Aaron.

Chapter 19

When Eva and Aaron arrived back home in Seattle, Gina told Eva Diamond was in labor. By this time Aaron knew Eva was assisting a student with her pregnancy.

"Aaron, Diamond is in labor and I'm going to the hospital to be with her. I don't know when I will be back but I will call you. Maria has dinner ready for you."

Eva kissed Aaron and left to go to the hospital. She was surprised and concerned that no one was with this 15-year-old student. She was all alone. Eva asked her where her mother was. Diamond said she had six kids and did not have a babysitter. Diamond said she was the oldest and normally watched her siblings, ages four to twelve, while her mother worked.

Eva called Aaron and let him know that she was going to be late getting home. "I'm going to help this child have this baby tonight Aaron." Aaron chuckled because Eva never had a baby.

"I watched YouTube and I read books. I know what to do." Aaron laughed even more.

Diamond was only three centimeters dilated when she arrived at the hospital. She was screaming like someone was killing her. Eva told her to breathe between contractions. The contractions were coming every seven to ten minutes. Every time a contraction happened Diamond would scream like someone was killing her.

"Diamond, did anyone prepare you for what's about to happen?"

"No!"

"Did you have prenatal care?"

"No one told me anything."

Eva remembered she told Gina that she would help her.

"I went to the doctor once after I talked to my principal. She told me you would help me through this, but I didn't want to bother a stranger. But I like you, though." Diamond screamed through another contraction.

"Wow! Well, first of all, you can handle this labor a little better if you don't scream during contractions. Try to breathe through them. I will help you. Sooner or later, they will come closer together and you will experience some pain but just continue to breathe through it."

"How many children do you have?" said Diamond.

"None! I watched the Baby Discovery Channel." They both laughed.

"There is no such thing as a Baby Discovery Channel."

Eva and Diamond bonded during the eight hours of labor. Eva asked the nurse if they could give her an epidural. The nurse said they wanted to wait until it was closer for her to push. After two more hours of screaming Eva demanded that they give the child some relief. They told Eva to step out while they gave the student the epidural. When Eva came back in the room Diamond was calm and ready to talk. Eva talked about her future wedding and they laughed about how big the head of the baby must be. Finally, the student was 10 centimeters. Eva held her legs while the doctor told her to push.

Diamond said, "This still hurts!!"

The doctor said, "It's just pressure. You are having a big baby... boy."

Her son finally arrived, weighing eight pounds, ten ounces. Diamond was relieved to have the baby. Eva held the baby and gave him to Diamond. The little boy was so beautiful and alert. Diamond kissed him on his forehead. "I think I'll name him Evan after you, Eva."

Eva gave the student her phone number and told her if she needed anything she would be there for her. "Just make sure you can put Supreme Court Justice after his name. There are too many crazy names out there."

They both laughed. A couple of days later Diamond called and said she needed a ride home and did not have a car seat. The hospital would not release her without a car seat. Eva and Aaron drove to the hospital to pick Diamond up. Diamond placed the baby in the car seat and sat next to her son. Eva noticed Diamond did not buckle up. "Buckle up, Diamond. Your baby is secure and you have to be too."

Diamond smiled and buckled up. "I never wear a seat belt, Miss Eva."

"Well, you need to start now. You need to buckle up anytime you get in a vehicle, Diamond. And make sure the baby is buckled in too."

"Yes ma'am."

They arrived at Diamond's house to see what else she needed. The home was small but clean, with three bedrooms for six kids, including Diamond. The house was organized and there were signs for chores for each kid on the refrigerator. Eva asked Diamond's mom if she could gift some furniture for Diamond and the children. Diamond's mother was overwhelmed with joy. They agreed to let Diamond have a room of her own with a crib for the baby, while the other five kids shared a room with a three-tier bunkbed for the older children and a queen bed for the two younger children. They were all two years apart. The four- and six-year-olds slept in the queen bed while the eight-, ten- and twelve-year-olds slept in the bunk bed.

Eva and Aaron purchased everything a newborn baby would need and placed it in Diamond's room.

They also purchased a refrigerator for Diamond to keep healthy snacks. Diamond thanked Eva for all her generosity.

Eva said, "All I want you to do is continue school and graduate on time. I will make sure you go to college. Just decide on the best career for you."

Diamond could not believe what had happened to her in just 72 hours. Diamond told Eva she was interested in nursing. Eva told Diamond there was always a need for nurses. It was a recession-proof career.

Diamond looked so confused. She had a baby boy plus five younger siblings and still had to finish school and go to college. Diamond wondered if she would make it. Eva told Diamond, "Call me if you need anything. I'll help you through this, Diamond. You are going to be okay. I know it's frightening but your baby is depending on you. Hold that baby tight and feed him when he's hungry and change him when he's wet. For the next few weeks that's all he will do is eat and sleep. Take care of yourself."

Aaron told Eva, "You know what, honey? You are so special. You treat people with kindness and grace. You never meet a stranger. People are drawn to you and every person you meet, including Rondell, you make a difference in their life. Rondell says now he has a sister. He said he wished you had a twin."

"Aaron, I treat people the way I want to be treated. I love helping others and watching people grow, especially my students. I pray every day for peace and happiness for all. This world would be a better place if everyone knew they are the one person that can make a difference. Diamond has a lot on her plate, but I'm convinced that she will be okay. She just needs some guidance."

Eva held Aaron's hand and walked back to the car and drove home. That night Diamond called Eva and Aaron and asked them to be godparents to Evan. They agreed.

Chapter 20

Eva was overjoyed to be Evan's godmother. She told Aaron when they got married the first thing she wanted to do was start a family. Aaron was excited about the possibility of being a dad. As Eva and Aaron continued their conversation, the phone rang. It was Gina asking Eva to speak at her honor roll assembly. The keynote speaker cancelled at the last minute.

"Eva! Can you please come and speak to our students during the honor roll assembly? My speaker cancelled at the last minute."

"Sure! What time do you need me to be there?"

"Ten a.m. tomorrow."

"Okay. Is it just for the honor roll students or are all your students going to be there?" "Just the honor roll."

"Let me suggest you invite everyone. I will write a speech that will address all of your students."

"Okay. Will do. But some of my students don't know how to behave during an assembly."

Eva laughed. "Really? Gina, I got this. Send them all. You'll be surprised how they behave when you set the expectation."

"Okay, my friend. I'll see you there."

That evening Eva sat down in her office and typed a 10-minute speech.

"Aaron! Do you want to come to the school tomorrow and hear my speech?"

"Of course, I would not miss it."

Eva decided to write a speech applauding the students for making the honor roll and encouraging the students who did not. She also thought it was important to address the violence in the world and send a message of hope and peace.

Chapter 21

It was a cold, rainy morning the day before Thanksgiving. Maria was in the kitchen making sweet potato pies and baking cakes. Eva was getting ready for her guests for Thanksgiving dinner.

"Okay Eva, how many guests are we expecting tomorrow?"

"Mom and Dad, Aaron and Rondell, Samantha, Angel and Lisa, Gina and her date, Mr. and Mrs. Kelly, Dan and Kiki. I invited Diamond and the baby but I don't think she's coming."

"Okay, so that's 15 people. I'll make the place cards. Who is Gina bringing?"

"I don't know. It's a mystery to me."

"Okay. Let's go over the menu again. We have turkey, ham, cornbread dressing, mashed potatoes, collard greens, sweet potatoes, corn, cranberry sauce, green beans, macaroni and cheese, and dinner rolls."

"Are you going to make the rolls from scratch?"

"Of course. I always do! For dessert, we will have sweet potato pie, apple cobbler, spice cake, and ambrosia."

"Our guests will arrive this evening so I want to have a hearty meal for them tonight." "Okay, Eva. I got this! You relax and wait for your fiancée."

Eva looked at her ring and said, "That's right. I have a fiancée. This will be our first Thanksgiving. We will have at least 50 more." Eva smiled at Maria. Maria did not know that a fortune teller predicted her long life with the man of her dreams.

Rondell and Aaron arrived with a lot of luggage.

"Did you guys plan to stay until Christmas? That's a lot of luggage." Maria wondered why they had two large suitcases each.

"No. We needed to have extra luggage for Black Friday."

"You guys go Black Friday shopping?"

"Yes. Every Friday after Thanksgiving. We shop all day. Parking is crazy but it's fun." "Wow. I never met a man that liked to shop the day after Thanksgiving."

Eva walked in and hugged her fiancée and Rondell. She showed Rondell to his room and asked how the flight was.

"The flight was great. It was only two hours and 45 minutes. I slept the entire time." Rondell smelled the aroma in the air of sweet potato pies. "Aaron, we are going to eat good this Thanksgiving."

"Yep. No hotel buffet this year." They both laughed and said, "Let's run, then. Anyone want to play spades?"

"Maybe later," Eva said.

That evening Eva and Maria played spades with Aaron and Rondell. Eva and Maria got 10 for 200 three times in a row. "Man!! They must be cheating. There is no way they can get 10 for 200 three times in a row."

"Hey man, Eva won every hand at blackjack. She said she was Lady Luck."

Eva and Maria gave each other a high five. After the third game Eva told Aaron she had a surprise for him. Eva walked over to her baby grand piano and played a song for Aaron. She played "Superstar/ Until you Come Back to Me."

As soon as the piano intro was played Aaron knew the song. He looked at Rondell. "Hey man, I didn't know she played the piano. Nothing surprises me anymore. My girl is great."

"You are so lucky, Aaron. She is smart, beautiful inside and out, talented, a gifted motivational speaker, a humanitarian, and she loves you, man. I'm so happy for you." Eva continued to play the song and Aaron began to sing and Rondell joined in. Maria was in the background with tears in her eyes, thinking, *Eva finally found love.*

The next morning all the guests started arriving around one o'clock to watch the football games. The doorbell rang. "We have another guest arriving, Eva."

Eva's parents and Aaron's parents showed up together. Next, Samantha, Angel and Lisa arrived a few minutes later. When Gina arrived, Eva opened the door and was surprised to see her police officer friend Shawn Gates. Eva introduced Shawn to everyone. Eva remembered Shawn's parents lived in Eva's new neighborhood. What she didn't know was they were next-door neighbors. Shawn's parents went to California for Thanksgiving so she invited him to dinner with her at Eva's. She knew Eva did not mind.

Thanksgiving dinner was always early, around 2:00 p.m. Maria set the table and everyone around the table said what they were thankful for. Eva said, "This is a very special Thanksgiving. I have found the love of my life and I'm so happy that I can share this day with our family and friends. God has blessed me with a wonderful man who is so kind and gentle. Aaron, I love you with all my heart and will love you forever. My mother told me patience is a virtue. I'm so glad I didn't settle and waited for you. You are my soul mate. God bless you and everyone here today. Let's bless this food and eat."

Chapter 22

As winter approached Eva and Aaron made plans to have a family vacation in Colorado for Christmas. Aaron had a house in Colorado Springs near a ski resort. It had 10 bedrooms and an exceptionally large family room with a fireplace that extended two stories. The open concept space was large enough to accommodate both their families. Aaron and Rondell arrived first and purchased a Christmas tree that was 12 feet tall.

"I think we should hire a professional decorator to trim this tree."

Rondell said, "No man. We need to dress it!"

"Rondell, you get dressed in the morning. We trim the Christmas tree!"

"Whatever, man." They both laughed. "Okay, let's get the decorations out of storage and call someone."

Aaron said, "Cool, my brother. When they arrive, they will feel the Christmas spirit in the house. And outside too."

A few hours later decorators arrived with lights for outside and inside. Wreaths were placed on all the doors. Poinsettias were placed on all the stairs and holly donned the rails of the stairs. Aaron hired a chef to bake cakes and cookies. Rondell and Aaron decided they would cook Christmas dinner.

"The ladies will be shocked that we are cooking Christmas dinner. It will be my first time, but I watched my mom cook all my life. I know what to do."

Rondell said, "Okay, my brother. Just tell me what to do and I will support you. I am not the cook… on the stove that is. I can grill my behind off though."

"Fact. Let's do this, man. First stop, grocery store."

Rondell said, "No man. We can have groceries delivered now. Let's put an online order in."

Aaron looked at Rondell and said, "Okay, man. I didn't want to drive in this snow anyway."

As the groceries arrived Aaron and Rondell organized the food and continued to watch the decorators. After everything was set, Aaron told Rondell he bought Eva a special gift for Christmas. "You know my fiancée loves handbags, so I bought her a black Burkin bag. I also bought her luggage for our next trip."

"Hey man, what's your next stop? South America? I should go with you all. Who knows, I may find my wife."

Aaron laughed and said, "No, my brother. Wherever we go, it will be a romantic trip with my queen."

The rest of the night Aaron sat around the fireplace with Rondell, laughing and talking about the good times they had in college and previous holidays.

Aaron said, "You know, when we lived in South Carolina, we used to play spades every Christmas Eve. My dad and his friends would come over and my mother would be baking cakes. She always made a pound cake, coconut cake, chocolate cake, fruit cake, and a spice cake. My dad would play cards with his partner and I swear he ran a 10 for 200 five times in a row."

"He had to be cheating," Eva and Maria said. They both laughed.

"Dude, your dad was cheating, man?"

"Yeah," they laughed, holding their stomachs. "It was crazy. I believe they had extra cards, man. One time I saw the Ace of Spades twice and they swore I didn't see it twice. They know how to stack the deck too, man."

Both families arrived at Aaron's house and celebrated Christmas together. They opened gifts on Christmas morning, watched the football game that afternoon and went to see a movie Christmas night. Every Christmas night Aaron's family saw a Christmas movie. Mr. Kelly tried to recall all the Christmas movies they had seen over the years. After the movies, everyone sat by the fireplace and sang Christmas carols. Ms. Kelly said it would be nice to have some grandchildren singing with them and opening gifts. Aaron and Eva looked at one another. Rondell said, "Okay. I'll have one soon." Everyone looked at Rondell and laughed.

Chapter 23

Eva flew back to Seattle after the Christmas holidays to pack for her trip with Aaron to New York City. Aaron had a gig in Philadelphia and was going to take a train to Grand Central Station while Eva flew to New York from Seattle.

Eva stood in the middle of Grand Central Station waiting for Aaron to arrive. Apparently, his train was delayed for an hour as Eva watched the arrival board every 10 minutes. Finally he arrived and Eva embraced Aaron with a big hug. Every time they were away from one another it was like the first time they met when they were together again. "What took your train so long? It was an hour late."

"It left Philly an hour late. I'm not sure why. They don't update like the airlines."

"Aaron, we have to go work out. I must have gained five pounds eating that Christmas dinner!"

"Eva, you changed the subject so fast, from a late train arrival to working out. We are in New York City.

There are lots of things to do. By the way, how's your blood sugar?"

"It was 108 this morning. My numbers are not too bad. Now who's changing the subject?"

"Let's go for a walk then. We can see some sights and go shopping for our next trip. It's cold outside but we can keep each other warm." Aaron and Eva walked around Times Square in New York. They arrived two days before New Year's Eve to enjoy the city for a few days before the big night. Eva had been to New York City many times but never during New Year's Eve. Aaron and Rondell had been to New York on New Year's Eve several times. "Eva, there is nothing like it. You will enjoy the evening."

On New Year's Eve Eva and Aaron ate dinner late and found a spot in Times Square to stand for the next few hours. They had on their New Year's Eve hats and glasses and loved the energy of the crowd. As the ball started to descend Eva looked at Aaron with love in her eyes and kissed him until the clock said midnight. Aaron stood behind Eva and looked up at the billboard that welcomed in the new year. "Today is the first day of the rest of our life, Eva Whitfield O'Sullivan."

Chapter 24

Eva and Aaron were back in Seattle for Valentine's Day. Eva glanced down at her engagement ring. She wondered what Aaron would give her for Valentine's Day. She knew he was a generous person and told him not to get her anything extravagant. Aaron already picked out her Valentine's gift while he was shopping in New York City while Eva was working out. He found a ten-stone cross pendant in white gold. Rondell told him she was going to love the gift. Eva told Gina that she was going to give Aaron something very special and straight from the heart.

"Eva, I am so happy for you. I wish I could find my soul mate. Maybe one day I will be just as happy as you are with the man of my dreams."

Eva had been thinking about Valentine's Day for a while. She gave Maria the night off so she could cook for Aaron. She broiled some lobster tails and cooked some chateaubriand with asparagus, broccoli and cauliflower with hollandaise sauce. She baked an apple cobbler for dessert. Eva purchased a black gift bag and placed three items in the bag. Each item represented a dream that Aaron wanted to come true. On February 14 at six o'clock Aaron arrived with flowers, candy and a gift for Eva. Eva met Aaron at the door and placed the flowers in a vase on the table where they were going to have dinner. "Where's Maria? I got her something too."

"I gave her the night off." Eva smiled.

"Does that mean you cooked dinner, Eva?"

"Yes, I did, my love. Your lady can cook too, baby!"

"I can't wait to eat, baby."

They sat down at the table in the dining room. Aaron loved the dinner as Tchaikovsky's Symphony No. 6 played.

After dinner Eva and Aaron sat by the fireplace in Eva's den. Aaron pulled out a gift bag with a little blue box from Tiffany's. Eva opened the box and saw the cross. "Aaron, it's beautiful!" Aaron fastened the necklace and kissed Eva on her shoulder. "Thank you, sweetheart."

Eva looked at Aaron and told him she had a speech to give. Aaron sat back and folded his arms. "Okay, baby. Let's go!"

"Aaron, you have my heart, my mind, and my soul. I love you more and more every day. I never thought I would be this happy. Yes, I loved my life before, but with you in my life... clearly I can see that my divine purpose is somehow connected to you. I love you so much. When I thought about what to give you on Valentine's Day, I couldn't think of one thing. I thought of three things. In this bag, I have three things that are very important and special for you and me. I'll let you take them out, one at a time."

Aaron looked at Eva and put his hand in the black gift bag, intentionally not looking at what he was grabbing until he pulled it out. It was coral and teal ribbon. "These are the colors of our wedding on the beach. We had a hard time deciding on the colors so I chose these and I hope you agree."

"Eva the colors are perfect for the backdrop of our wedding on the beach this summer. I love it."

The second item was a pair of blue and pink baby booties. "This represents the child that we will have. It doesn't matter whether it's a boy or girl. I have the spare shoe ready to make the set." Aaron smiled with love in his eyes. He pulled the final item gift out of the bag: two tickets to Rio de Janeiro, Brazil. "Rio is a place we have never been and I have always dreamed of going there. I always wanted to go there to see one of the seven wonders of the world, the Corcovado. I've already planned our spring trip to Rio."

"Eva, I love you so much!" Eva and Aaron kissed.

"Aaron, I have one more thing to give you." Eva wrote a poem for Aaron.

He read it silently. When he looked up he had tears in his eyes. "No one has ever written anything for me. I'm always writing for someone else. This means so much to me. Thank you, Eva." Aaron put his head down and stared at the poem. He placed the ribbon and the baby booties on each corner of the framed poem. He said, "I'll remove them when each dream comes true." Aaron looked at Eva. "You gave me all of my dreams in a little black bag. As each of these dreams come true, I'll replace them with new dreams. I love you, Eva. Until the end of time, I'll always love you."

Eva and Aaron walked to the deck that overlooked the lake. Eva rested her head on his shoulders and Tchaikovsky continued to play.

Chapter 25

Eva and Aaron's birthdays were so close together, they decided to have one party on a ski trip to Vail, Colorado. Eva didn't know that Rondell had a vacation home in Vail and Aaron had invited Gina to come to Vail and join them for a small birthday party. Aaron also arranged for Eva's parents and his parents to attend the party in Vail.

"Rondell, I pray that I-70 stays open. I heard a storm is coming so we are leaving earlier than expected."

"No worries, my brother. You have the key. Enjoy your alone time with Eva. I'm working on a painting for her house. The lake and her neighborhood has inspired me." "Rondell, you have painted for a minute. I'm proud of you, my brother."

Eva and Aaron flew in a private plane to a local airport. When they arrived at the house Eva was really impressed by the art deco. She asked Aaron who the house belonged to.

"I will give you one guess, Eva."

Eva looked surprised. She walked around and saw a picture of Aaron and Rondell on the slopes. "Rondell owns this house?"

"Yep! We come here all the time in the winter. Sometimes we come in the fall and just hang out. It's a great place to write music."

"And paint, I guess. Look at this art. Rondell is amazing. A lot of this is impressionism. Like Monet, Rondell likes to paint what he sees in nature. This picture of a sole skier on the slopes is amazing."

Eva looked at Aaron. "Is there something wrong, Aaron?"

Aaron was holding his head as if it hurt. "I'm okay. Maybe I had too much to drink on the plane. I feel a little nausea too." Aaron went to the restroom and threw up.

"Aaron, let me get you some water. You need to hydrate, sweetheart." Eva rushed to take care of Aaron. She noticed his balance was off a little. "Aaron, maybe you should not ski tomorrow if you aren't feeling well."

"I'll be okay, Eva."

That evening Eva and Aaron went to the ski slopes and decided to sit by a fireplace in a cabin and drink apple cider. Aaron was feeling better so they took a sleigh ride together. "Aaron, it's beautiful out here. What a great idea to celebrate our birthdays together in Colorado."

Aaron smiled and thought about the big surprise he had for Eva. She didn't know her parents were coming. She was just expecting Rondell and Gina. When they arrived back at Rondell's house Gina was there, and Maria Sanchez too. Aaron invited her to plan the party and menu for their birthdays. Maria was more than willing to assist. Eva was excited to see her assistant and her best friend. When Aaron saw Rondell, they gave each other the Q sign and said, "Friendship is essential to the soul." They hugged it out and sat down for a drink.

The next morning Aaron took Eva out to lunch in town while her parents and his parents arrived. When they arrived back to the house everyone was there. When Eva opened the door, her parents said, "Surprise! Happy birthday!!"

Eva was thrilled. All of her dreams were coming true.

Chapter 26

The next day Aaron and Rondell went skiing at the local resort. Eva and Gina decided to stay at the house and plan for the wedding. Eva decided on 25 guests each for the wedding. Gina would be her maid of honor and Rondell would be the best man. She didn't want to have bridesmaids or groomsmen. She wanted to keep it simple, with just close family and friends. She decided to have an evening wedding, just before the sunset. "This is going to be a lovely wedding on the beach with coral and teal colors. I can hardly wait until June 10."

The wedding date was set. Now they had to select the invitations. Although it would be a destination wedding, there was a lot of work to do.

Aaron and Rondell were skiing on the slopes. Aaron's dad was with Mr. O'Sullivan in the cabin, smoking cigars and having drinks. All of a sudden they looked out the window and saw flashing emergency lights. As they looked closer they saw Aaron being placed on a gurney in an ambulance. They rushed out of the cabin and asked Rondell what happened. "Aaron said his head felt light." They were both skiing. "Aaron fell and slid down a small hill and hit a tree." It didn't appear that he broke his legs or arms. Aaron was unconscious for a few minutes and when he woke up he said his head was hurting. Mr. O'Sullivan immediately called Eva and told her to meet them at the hospital. "Aaron had an accident, Eva. He's okay but he's on his way to the hospital."

Chapter 27

Eva went to the hospital and spoke to the doctor in charge. He asked her questions about Aaron's condition prior to the accident.

"Aaron was having headaches yesterday, and he threw up. I told him he should not go skiing if he didn't feel well."

Aaron's dad and mom told the doctor Aaron survived cancer as a child. The doctor told Aaron's parents that the CT scan and lab test revealed a brain bleed. Aaron's doctor said he would also have to have emergency surgery to remove the blood as soon as possible.

Eva looked at Rondell and her parents. "I knew there was something wrong yesterday. But I know in my heart, he will be okay. He has to be. We have a long life to live." Eva remembered that the psychic told her she would have a long life with the man she loved.

Eva had a few minutes to spend with Aaron before he was rolled into surgery. She told him that he was going to be okay and when he woke up she would be there for him. Aaron's mom hugged Eva and told her, "He will be okay."

Eva looked in Aaron's mom's eyes and said, "I know. I have faith. It's not his time." Everyone went to the chapel in the hospital and prayed for Aaron's health.

Aaron's surgery was six hours long. His family patiently waited for him to return to the recovery room. The doctor came out and told the family the surgery was a success; however, he would not have visitors in the recovery room. They were wheeling him to ICU. Eva wondered if the surgery was a success, why was he going to ICU?

Aaron's parents let Eva in the room first. Aaron was awake but unable to talk. She called his name and he looked at her but could only moan. Eva asked the nurse what was wrong with him. The nurse said, "He's still under anesthesia and kind of out of it." Eva looked at Aaron again. Aaron turned his head and looked at her. He moaned again. Eva started to cry and left the room. Mr. and Mrs. Kelly went in next. All of a sudden a team of doctors rushed in the room. Aaron's blood pressure was 210/108. He was trying to get up from the bed and struggling to breathe. They gave him meds to get the blood pressure down and placed a machine in his room to determine if he was having seizures.

The doctors came out to talk to the family. They decided to place Aaron on a medical ventilator because he was unable to breathe on his own. Eva fell into Rondell's arms and cried hysterically. After the ventilator was hooked up Eva asked the nurse if she could stay with him.

Rondell made a few calls to cancel Aaron's shows. He told Eva she could stay at his house in Vail as long as she needed to. Eva looked outside. The snow was falling. She realized today was her birthday and her biggest gift in life was in the hospital. Eva had faith. She knew he wouldn't die. She prayed for his healing. That night Eva slept in ICU in Aaron's room. She talked to him all night about their future. "Aaron, you have to wake up. You have not met my mother yet. We have a trip to Rio this spring, and we have our wedding in June. Do you hear me, Aaron? You have to wake up. It's not your time. Now wake up and breathe on your own." Eva reached over Aaron and sang to him.

Aaron's family was at the hospital every day for two weeks when suddenly he woke up. The doctor took him off the ventilator and Aaron started to talk. "What happened to me?" Eva told him he had brain surgery. His prognosis was good. They removed the bleed but he had seizures after the surgery.

Aaron was moved from ICU to a regular room. The day he was moved to a regular room Aaron became non-responsive. He would not react to light, sound or pain. Eva wondered if he was in a coma. One of the nurses asked the doctor why he was moved if he was non-responsive. Eva told the nurse he was okay and talking just a few moments before he was moved. "Hang in there, Aaron. I'm not going anywhere. I'm with you."

The nurse started to stimulate Aaron's chest. "Mr. Kelly, wake up. Mr. Kelly? Aaron. Aaron, squeeze my hand."

Aaron squeezed the nurse's hand slightly. Eva was watching him. "Aaron! Open your eyes." Aaron opened his eyes. "If you can hear me, nod your head." Aaron nodded his head slightly.

Eva knew he was in there somewhere. Eva called all her friends to pray for Aaron's complete healing. He was on every prayer list in Seattle, Las Vegas, Savanah, and Columbia. For the next few days Aaron had moments of non-responsiveness due to seizures. The doctors prescribed seizure medication for him. Finally, after four weeks in the hospital, Aaron had a miraculous recovery. He could walk, talk, feed himself and sing. The headaches were gone. Aaron walked out of the hospital with Eva and took the next flight to Las Vegas.

Eva stayed with Aaron over the Easter holiday. They went to church on Palm Sunday and Easter Sunday. Rondell cooked Easter dinner for them. After dinner Eva got a phone call from her mother. Daisy Whitfield, her birth mother, was dying. She was in the end stages of renal disease.

"Aaron, my mother is extremely ill. We have to go see her."

"Mrs. O'Sullivan?"

"No, Daisy Whitfield, my birth mother."

Rondell said, "I'm in. I'll go with you. Do you need a private plane?"

Eva and Aaron looked at Rondell and smiled.

"Hey, I have my pilot's license now!"

"Rondell!! I'm not flying anywhere with you behind the wheel!"

Everyone was laughing as Rondell said, "I'm just kidding. I do have access to a private plane, though."

Aaron said, "We can fly into Charleston and drive an hour and a half to Salters."

Maria booked the flight for the next day.

Chapter 28

Aaron, Rondell and Eva drove an hour and a half to Salters, SC. Maria called Ms. Whitfield's nurse and housekeeper to let them know that Eva was coming. Ms. Whitfield's housekeeper prepared three rooms for the guests to stay at the estate where Daisy lived. As they drove through town they saw signs: Whitfield shoeshine, Whitfield post office, and Whitfield grocery. None of the buildings were open, as they were built in the 1800s. The only thing new was the lock on the grocery store. Aaron crossed a railroad track and saw the old train station on the left. He wondered where the citizens of the town ate when they went out. The nearest town was Kingstree. The trees had moss hanging from them and there was a lot of farmland. Eva noticed a couple driving a golf cart. As they passed by they waved to them. "Friendly folks around here," said Rondell. "It's so quiet and peaceful around here."

They drove down a long gravel road and saw a huge mansion at the end. There were large trees everywhere and there was a lake in the back yard. They passed what looked like a burial ground. The house had a large porch with rocking chairs. The setting was picturesque. It was so beautiful, Eva just looked in awe.

As she walked into the parlor, she looked up at the details in the ceiling. It looked like artwork was everywhere. Eva was greeted by her mother's house-keeper, who reminded her of Maria, her personal assistant. She gave her a hug as if she knew her. Eva looked around and saw a lot of pictures of her. Her baby pictures and every school picture from grades K-12 was there. Her three graduation pictures were there also. Juanita, Daisy's housekeeper, told Eva that her mother was at every graduation. Eva was amazed. She felt love in the house. "Where is she?"

The nurse opened her hand and showed her the way to Daisy's bedroom on the first floor. As Eva walked in the room she couldn't help but look at the impressionist paintings on the wall. Eva said to herself, *I must have gotten my love of art from my mother.* Eva walked over to her mother and said, "Mother? I'm here. I'm so happy to meet you." "Eva, you are my only child. I don't have long to live but I want you to know that I love you. When I die, I have willed my estate to you. There is a lot of history on this land and I want you to learn about where you come from. Is Aaron here?"

"Yes."

"Well, bring him in here."

"Aaron! My mother wants to meet you."

"Don't forget Rondell."

"Mother, you know about Rondell?"

"Well, they said they were making up three rooms so I figured Rondell was coming." Daisy smiled. She was very frail yet very beautiful. She looked like she weighed 95 pounds. Her eyes were very big and her cheeks were sunken. Eva could tell she was really sick.

Rondell walked in behind Aaron and said, "Hello Miss Daisy!" Rondell was always cheerful and a comedian at times.

"Hi Rondell! I'm glad you are here. Make yourself at home. Aaron, I heard you like sweet potato pie."

"Yes ma'am."

"Well, I made you one." Aaron looked at Eva with his eyebrows raised. "Oh, I may be ill, but I can still cook."

Eva smiled at her mother and asked the men if she could speak to her mom alone. Aaron and Rondell walked out and sat on the front porch. Eva stayed and talked to her mother for six hours. Daisy told Eva that she had hundreds of tapes of oral history outlining the history of the Abercromby family, who had settled in Williamsburg County in SC in the late 1700s. Eva was so amazed at how sharp her mother's mind was.

"Tell me about them, Mother."

Daisy smiled when she called her Mother. Daisy told Juanita to sit her up a little and she sipped on a cup of water. "In the late 1700s the Abercromby family emigrated from Scotland. They settled in Williamsburg County. Your great-great-great-grandfather, John Abercromby, was born in 1790 and died in 1890. He was a very wealthy man and owned lots of land around here. He was a tobacco and cotton farmer. He married Audrey Johnson in 1815. She was an English descendant of the former governor. They had six children. Two died during childbirth; two died of malaria. There was a lot of disease back then due to the mosquitoes in the marshlands. Two children survived, Peter Abercromby Jr., born 1817, and Samuel Abercromby, born 1816. Samuel Abercromby married Anna Calhoun Locke in 1835 and they had their only son, Arthur Abercromby, in 1841. He was promiscuous with the slaves and his mother Anna was upset with him often. She kept a lot of the slaves in the house, away from her son.

"After the slaves were freed, some stayed on the farm and worked as sharecroppers and house maids. Arthur was smitten by a maid named Cecelia. Anna Calhoun Locke wrote in her Bible that Arthur Abercromby fathered Maybelle Wilson with Cecelia Wilson. No one believed it was consensual. Maybelle was born with hazel eyes and blonde hair. She passed for white. Arthur's brother, Samuel Abercromby, took the baby from both of them and raised her in his house. He had no children because his wife was barren. Maybelle was treated like a princess. The diaries are in that chest over there."

Eva looked around with tears in her eyes. "Mother, when was she born?"

"In 1896. March 5, 1896. She lived to be 100. She died in 1996. Your great-great-great-grandfather Peter lived to be 100 too. When Maybelle was 24 the family home burned down. No one knows why. The Abercrombys rebuilt the house when Maybelle married George Whitfield in 1916. The Whitfields were prominent farmers in Williamsburg County. On March 6, 1926, my mother Selena Wilson Whitfield was born, in this house, in this room. Your grandparents died in 2011 and 2012. Daddy just could not live without Momma. He died of a broken heart. Momma had kidney disease and high blood pressure. I was born on February 27, 1948 in this house. Someone recently told me the doula that delivered me still lives on the other side of the bridge. Eva, all of this family history is true and documented in Bibles, journals, and diaries. I started recording these stories years ago.

"All of the graves are outside in the garden cemetery. We've been buried in the family plot outside since 1817 when the first two children died. The family has always been prosperous. During the Great Depression, they lived off the land."

Eva laid her hand on her mother's and said she couldn't wait to start reading. Daisy appeared to be tired and fell asleep. Juanita walked in and showed Eva to her room. Eva lay on her bed and looked at the ceiling. She looked around the room and said, "This really feels like home."

The next morning Eva walked with Daisy as she pushed her in a wheelchair. Daisy showed Eva the property and took her to visit her father's grave.

"My dad is buried on your property?"

"Of course."

Eva smiled as she recognized her mom said of course, just like she did.

"This is your dad's grave. He never knew I was pregnant before he died. I didn't find out until later."

Eva started to tell her that she met her dad in heaven but decided not to. "Tell me about my dad, Mother. What was he like?"

"Your dad was an amazing person. We grew up together. We used to walk around with bare feet and run through the tobacco fields. We went to Sunday School and church together, and we went swimming together in the lake. We always knew we wanted to go to college together, but his dad wanted him to join the Army and travel the world. Anthony had a different plan. He wanted to open a law firm with me. I always told him it would have to be named Whitfield and Gaskins, Attorneys at Law. He laughed because I always loved my last name.

"His dad was friends with the Abercrombys. In the 1800s the Whitfields were purchased as slaves by the Abercrombys. After the Thirteenth Amendment, Peter Abercromby gave all his slaves an opportunity to become sharecroppers. Most left for the North. A lot of Whitfields moved to Philadelphia, New York,

Connecticut, and Vermont. Some actually moved to Canada. When we were young, he did not go to school in the spring; he had to work in the fields. So I taught him everything I learned in school. Your great-grandmother Selena kept a library in this house. You will find books that are priceless. Many a day Anthony and I would sit on a swing on the back porch reading and writing. I remember one time Anthony was just sitting down, looking at all the trees and the water. He said to me, 'One day we will have kids that run in these fields, play in this water, and swing on this swing. One day, I will be reading the great books to my grandchildren on the Saturday evenings after dinner.' He would look at me and tell me how much he loved me."

"Wow, he was a romantic person."

"Oh yes. You know, we got married on this property in the garden. We wrote our own vows. We were two college students, but we didn't want to wait to get married. Our love was very pure and we longed for one another. I always loved art as well as my great-grandmother. Everyone wanted to gift us art as a wedding present."

Eva asked her mother about the artwork in her home. She told her she purchased most from an art dealer in Savannah; however, some were wedding gifts. Eva told her mother she loved art too.

"There is so much art in our home, you can open a museum. The Abercrombys were art collectors."

"Mother? When was dad's birthday?"

"One day after mine. February 28, 1948."

Eva smiled. "Aaron's birthday is close to mine too." Eva started to think about all of the information she received from her mother. She thought about the number of relatives that lived to be 100 and how the psychic told her she would live a long life with the one she loved. Eva began to feel like she was home. She wished she had met her mother long before now. She was thankful to have the time with her before she passed away.

That evening Eva, Aaron, Rondell, and Daisy sat in the library while Daisy told the others about the history of the family. Aaron talked about the times he passed the exit for Williamsburg County and never knew how much history was there. Aaron said, "It's amazing how I have traveled all over the world and met the girl of my dreams." He professed his love to Eva in front of her mother and best friends.

Eva enjoyed the time that she spent with her birth mother but knew she had to get back to prepare for her trip to Rio. Eva kissed her mother goodbye and somehow knew she would never see her again. Before Eva left, Daisy said, "You have a gift. You see things no one else does. Use your gift to help others see the light."

Eva smiled at her mother. She nodded her head. For some reason, she believed Daisy had the gift too.

The next day Eva, Aaron, and Rondell drove back to Charleston and flew back to Las Vegas. Eva called her mother and told her she met Daisy and the visit was wonderful. She let her mother know that Daisy was very ill and she should visit soon too.

When they arrived back in Las Vegas Rondell went to his art studio to work, inspired by the paintings in Daisy's house.

Chapter 29

Eva had researched tourist attractions in Rio prior to her trip with Aaron. She knew she wanted to see the Corcovado, Sugar Loaf Mountain, and the world famous Copacabana Beach. On the plane to Rio Aaron and Eva were in first class drinking champagne. They were celebrating Aaron's full recovery and getting ready for their wedding. The Save the Date card was delivered in December, before Christmas. They had to select the wedding invitations and get them in the mail. When the plane landed, they were driven to their hotel downtown right on the beach. Aaron wanted to go to a shop that made gemstones out of igneous rocks. He planned to purchase a gift for Eva and give it to her as a wedding gift.

The first day in Rio De Janeiro, Brazil they rested from the long flight. The second day they planned a trip to the Corcovado and Sugar Loaf Mountain. The minivan picked them up from their hotel. They met another couple that were there on their honeymoon. Lela and Leon Love were born and raised in New York City. "Love was in the air." The couple lived in Manhattan and worked in real estate. They told Eva and Aaron that they left town during New Years and spent New Year's Eve in Brazil at Copacabana Beach. Aaron and Eva told their new friends about their New York experience on New Year's Eve.

Aaron said, "It's nothing like Vegas, though. They shut down the strip."

"We need to get an apartment in New York City, Aaron. I love New York."

"On your next visit, we can show you a few apartments," said Leon.

"Honey, I have the perfect building with great views of Central Park."

"Yes! I'd love that. We took a stroll in Central Park last winter. I can use that park for my morning jog," said Ava.

"Okay. We will visit soon. We have to get married first. We still have a lot to do." "That's why we have a wedding planner, Aaron."

Both couples were happy and held hands while they walked to the Corcovado. They decided to take the stairs to the Christ the Redeemer statue. As Eva walked up the stairs with Aaron she noticed an older woman barely making it up the stairs. The lady would take one step and stop. Then she would sit down and get up again. "Aaron, look at that lady. She should have taken the elevator."

"Yeah, she looks so tired, Eva."

"You guys walk on. I'm going to help her." Eva walked over to the elderly lady. The woman was bent over and held her heart. She had on a white dress with a colorful scarf around her neck. Her skin was wrinkled and bronzed from the sun. She had hazel eyes and white hair. "Hi! My name is Eva. Can I help you up these stairs?"

The lady looked at Eva and said, "I have a bad heart but I'm going to make it up these stairs."

"You can take the elevator if you'd like."

"No. I'm strong enough to make it up these stairs. My name is Ursula. I live in Sao Paulo."

Eva walked up the stairs with Ursula. Ursula told Eva she was 92 years old and used to be an artist until her arthritis set in. She told her many of her works were in museums in Sao Paulo. She also had a studio where she continued to teach young artists. Ursula was an impressionist. She was born December 5, 1926, the same day that Claude Monet died. Her mother was an artist, as well as her dad. Her dad studied art in France in the late 1800s. That was where he met his wife. Ursula told Eva she had all of her father's works in her studio. As they continued to climb the stairs Eva was intrigued by Ursula's story and life. Ursula told Eva she had a sister who lived in Sydney, Australia. She had not seen her in 30 years, since her brother's death from pneumonia.

Eva told Ursula she visited Sydney last year. "Is your sister an artist too?"

"No. She is a psychic. She has a gift to talk to the deceased and she can tell the future. She's always had the gift, since birth."

Eva looked at Ursula and noticed a mole on the right side of her chin. Could the psychic she met in the Blue Mountains be Ursula's sister? Or was this just a coincidence? Eva and Ursula continued to walk up the stairs. "How old is your sister?"

"She's 72. We are two decades apart. I'd love to see her again before I die."

Eva's mind was going around in circles. When Eva reached the top of the statue she looked at Ursula and asked her, "What is your sister's name?"

"Nicolette."

Eva was in shock. She pulled out her phone and found the picture of the lady she met in the Blue Mountains. "Is this your sister?"

Ursula was speechless. She stared at the photo and one tear dropped from her eye to her cheek to her lap. Eva knew the answer by the expression on her face. "Yes. That is my sister."

Eva called Aaron on her cell and said, "Aaron, you are never going to believe this. The little lady that I met in the Blue Mountains—this woman is her sister. It's a small world!" Eva was a thinker. Why did she meet the psychic? Why did she meet Ursula? There were no mistakes in life. Everything happened for a reason. The idea of six degrees of separation was a reality. Why did she meet these women? Eva wondered how the two could connect again. She didn't have an address or number, just a picture.

Ursula invited Eva and Aaron to her hometown. Eva told Ursula about their love story and how she met her sister. Aaron wrote down all of Ursula's information and let her know that he would find Nicolette and they would be reunited. Eva and Aaron were thrilled to discover that the psychic she met was going to reunite with her sister. After a week in Brazil, Eva and Aaron flew to Rome. Her birth mother was still alive and she spoke to her daily by phone.

Chapter 30

Traveling around the world with Aaron was exciting and adventurous for Eva. Eva had been to Rome before and always said she would return with her true love. She threw a coin in the Fontaine de Trevi and prayed for finding her soul mate. Now she was on a plane to Rome with Aaron.

When they arrived in Rome a car was waiting for them. Maria had arranged for their accommodations and travel. On the drive to their hotel Eva said, "Okay, Aaron. Tomorrow we are going to the Coliseum, Vatican City, Sistine Chapel, St. Peter's Basilica, and the National Museum of Castel Sant'Angelo. Tonight, let's go to dinner and rest from that long flight."

"I've got a surprise for you, Eva."

"Don't tell me you have a house in Italy too."

"No, but we are going to Florence on a day trip this week. Gina and Rondell are going to meet us there. You know Rondell loves museums."

"That's great. Are Rondell and Gina an item now?"

"Not hardly. Rondell is not ready for a commitment. He's not ready to settle down but Gina is a fine person. I know she will find someone who loves her just as much as I love you."

"You know, Aaron, we are really blessed to have great friends and family. To travel anywhere we want to go and be able to share our gifts with the world."

"I feel you. I feel so good when I look into an audience and see the concertgoers having a good time."

"It's the same when I give a speech. I look into the audience and the head nods affirming what I am saying let me know they get it."

Eva began to think about Ursula. She wondered how she could get the sisters together again. Aaron told Eva they would figure it out. "Let's enjoy Rome for now." Aaron hugged his fiancée as they walked in their hotel room.

Chapter 31

The next stop on their European tour was London. When they arrived, the weather was foggy and cold. Their hotel suite was not ready. They stored their luggage at the hotel and took a taxi to go shopping. "Where would you like to go?" the taxi driver said.

"To the mall, please." Eva and Aaron were excited to go shopping in London. Eva had been to London for a conference but never shopped or toured London.

After a few minutes the taxi driver said, "We are here." Eva and Aaron did not pay attention to their surroundings. They paid the taxi driver and got out of the car. They looked around for shops but all they saw were gates and guards.

"Eva! This is not the mall, it's Buckingham Palace."

Eva looked at the palace and said, "Of course. This is the mall. Like the mall in Washington, DC."

Aaron laughed. "Well, the queen isn't expecting us so let's take a taxi to some stores." "Wait, let's take some pictures. Maybe we can see the Changing of the Guard. It takes place around 10:45am. Its 10:40am now." Aaron agreed and they watched the 45-minute ceremony. "Mom and dad are going to love these pictures."

Chapter 32

After a week in London, Aaron and Eva flew to Paris. When they arrived, their luggage was nowhere to be found. This was the first trip where their luggage was lost. The agent at the airport assured them it would be on the next flight and he would have it delivered to them. When they arrived at the hotel Aaron went to the concierge desk to book a dinner cruise on the Seine River. Aaron and Eva couldn't wait to arrive in Paris and speak the language when touring and ordering food. Eva wondered if Rondell would show up at the Louvre. She loved the way Aaron and his best friend were like brothers and hung out together. Eva felt like Rondell was her brother she never had. Rondell was very funny and always made her laugh. As she looked out her bedroom window in the hotel, she could see the Eiffel Tower. It was only a short walk. She decided to walk over with Aaron and when they returned, hopefully their luggage would be there.

The flowers around the Eiffel Tower were so beautiful. Aaron took pictures of Eva and they took selfies of themselves. "Eva, this time next month, we will be husband and wife. I can hardly wait to call you Mrs. Kelly."

Eva looked at Aaron and said, "Of course. I can hardly wait too."

They stopped for some ice cream on the way back to the hotel. They decided to go on a tour to the home of Claude Monet in Giverny, France. As soon as they booked the tour, their luggage showed up. Aaron and Eva vacationed in France for a week. Eva said, "On the next trip to France let's go to Monaco."

Aaron agreed. Finally, they flew back home to prepare for their wedding in Punta Cana.

Chapter 33

Eva and Aaron were excited about their wedding day. On the flight to Punta Cana Eva had more champagne than usual. Aaron smiled at his future bride letting loose a little bit. Maria made all the accommodations for everyone, including the guests.

Everyone settled in their suites after the parties. The wedding was scheduled for sunset the next day. It was a beautiful day on the beach. Aaron wondered how he would handle not seeing Eva all day. Gina, Sam, Lisa, Maria, and Ms. O'Sullivan went to the spa and shopping. Aaron, the colonel, Mr. Kelly, Shorty, Shawn, and Rondell went to play golf. Aaron planned to have a bachelor party the night before the wedding.

Eva decided to wear her birth mother Daisy's wedding dress on her special day. Maria made sure her trousseau was together. Years ago, Eva's birth mother sent her wedding dress to Mrs. O'Sullivan. Gina bought her a new veil for the dress. She also bought her a blue garter. Samantha let Eva borrow her diamond necklace. When Eva looked in her room there was a set of Louis Vuitton luggage that Aaron bought, filled with her favorite things. Aaron knew Eva's style.

That night at the bachelorette party Lisa told Eva anytime they were ready, she would carry their baby. Eva was thrilled at the thought of having a child with the love of her life; however, she told Lisa she was going to try the old-fashioned way on her honeymoon. They both smiled as Eva winked.

On Eva and Aaron's wedding day the weather was ideal. The ceremony was set for sunset. There was no rain in the forecast. Eva woke up that morning watching the sunrise and playing her favorite song. She sipped her tea and began to think about her life. She smiled and prayed to God for a healthy marriage, full of love and peace.

She turned off her music as she heard someone singing outside her window. She lifted the window and a man was singing, "This is why I love you." Another person held a sign saying, "A gift from Aaron." Then there was a knock on the door with a note from Aaron: "Today is the first day of the rest of our life. I love you, Eva Whitfield O'Sullivan. You are my everything. As we continue this journey of love, let us always remember how we met as we set out to take on the world and find our divine purpose together. I love you, baby." Eva kissed the letter and tears rolled down her cheek.

The wedding party arrived at the venue and patiently waited for Eva's arrival. All of a sudden they heard Canon in D. Colonel O'Sullivan walked Eva down the aisle. Eva carried white calla lilies. Eva walked over to Aaron and Aaron tilted his head to the side. He looked into her eyes and mouthed, "I love you." The pastor officiated the ceremony right on time. As soon as she pronounced them man and wife the sun set. It was the most beautiful wedding of the day, the wedding coordinator said.

As Eva and Aaron walked down the aisle she noticed Ursula and Nicolette were there. Aaron hired a private investigator to find Nicolette and arranged for them to attend the wedding. Daisy was too ill to attend; however, Rondell had a videographer record the ceremony just for Daisy. Eva and Aaron recorded a video message to Daisy. The wedding was streamed to Daisy so she could see her only child on her wedding day.

As Daisy watched the wedding and video message, she closed her eyes. The next day she passed away in the morning as the sun was coming up. Her nurse was by her side as she said her final words. "I love Eva."

Daisy left a note for her housekeeper and nurse not to tell Eva she passed while she was on her honeymoon. The O'Sullivans were told but Eva would not get the message until after their honeymoon.

Chapter 34

When Eva and Aaron returned from their honey-moon, they were informed by the O'Sullivans that Daisy Whitfield passed away. She left a letter for Eva and willed her entire estate to Eva. Eva and Aaron, along with the rest of the family and friends, went to Salters, SC for the funeral. The church was small and the wooden floors shook while the chorus sang "Sweet, Sweet Spirit." Daisy's nurse spoke at her funeral and her old friend Pastor Brown gave the eulogy. Eva wanted to speak but she was too upset to talk. She cried in Aaron's arms.

After the funeral, everyone met at the mansion, which now belonged to Eva. Daisy was buried in the family plot on the land and Eva placed the last white flowers on her grave. As Eva walked inside the house the guests were staring at her. Eva looked just like her birth mother.

Eva pulled Aaron aside and said, "We should come here every summer with our children. There is so much history here. I want to know everything about the Whitfields and the Gaskins."

Aaron kissed Eva on her forehead and said, "Whatever you want, my dear."

Rondell was sitting on the sofa in the parlor, looking at guests as they arrived and left. He kept moving his head back and forth. Suddenly, he saw Ursula and Nicolette. They could not make the funeral but they were able to make the repast. Their plane was delayed six hours. Rondell walked Ursula and Nicolette to Eva and Aaron. Nicolette looked at Eva and immediately knew something was wrong. It wasn't her mother's death. There was something else on Eva's mind.

Chapter 35

Eva and Aaron flew back to Seattle three weeks after Daisy's funeral. They stayed in SC to take care of the estate, as Eva was the executor. Maria Sanchez met them at the door and gave her condolences. Rondell went back to Las Vegas and the O' Sullivans went to Charleston to see some friends. When Eva went to sleep that evening she told Aaron this was the first night in their home as husband and wife. She felt like she should do something special; however, she was emotionally drained.

Eva and Aaron were home for 12 weeks when Eva woke up one morning very tired and was not feeling well. "Let's just get some rest, and tomorrow is a new day."

"Okay, Eva. Let me run a bubble bath for you. I'll get you some tea too."

Eva smiled at Aaron, thinking, *I married an amazing man*. After Eva's bath, she went to sleep while

Aaron was working on a song he was writing for Eva. Eva tossed and turned all night.

When Aaron came to bed Eva was sweating and tossing and turning. Aaron tried to comfort Eva but she was struggling with something. Finally, the next morning, Eva sat up and called Diamond's name.

"What's going on with Diamond?" Aaron said.

"I don't know but something is wrong. Evan. Oh no, Evan!!"

"Eva what is going on in your mind right now?"

"There is going to be an accident, Aaron. I have to warn Diamond!" Eva called Diamond and there was no answer. She called Diamond's mother and there was no answer. Aaron told Eva he would drive her to Diamond's house if she really was concerned.

Eva jumped out of bed and said, "Let's go." Eva grabbed her coat. She kept on her pajamas and ran out of the house with Aaron.

As Aaron drove down the hill and through the city, Eva began to cry. "Hang on, sweetheart. We will get there." Eva continued to cry. "I think it's too late Aaron. My heart hurts."

As they pulled up to Diamonds house, a police officer was at the door already. When Diamond's mother opened the door, the police told her that Diamond was in a car accident and was in critical condition in the hospital.

Eva didn't wait to speak to anyone. She told Aaron, "Let's go!" When Eva arrived at the hospital she went straight to ICU. Diamond was there in a coma. She was driving without a seatbelt and hit a tree. She flew out the window and broke her neck and several bones. Evan was in the car seat in the back of the car. Evan was fine.

Eva asked the nurse, "Where is her baby?" The nurse asked if she was family. "Listen! I helped deliver that baby; of course I'm family." The nurse took her to the room where baby Evan was sleeping peacefully. The doctor came in and said the baby was fine. "Not even a scratch."

"Can I pick him up?"

"Sure."

Eva washed her hands and picked up baby Evan. She held him tight and looked at Aaron. "Honey, hold Evan. I've got to talk to Diamond." When she went back in Diamond's room, they were covering her up. Diamond passed away from her injuries, "NO!! Give me a minute with her." Eva pulled the sheet back and apologized to Diamond. "I had this funny feeling for several days now and I didn't know what it meant until last night. If only I could have reached you. I knew you were in trouble. Diamond, I told you to wear your seatbelt at all times! Diamond. Diamond!!!! Oh God, why Diamond?"

Aaron came in the room and hugged Eva. Eva got sick and threw up. Suddenly Eva passed out. Eva was seen in the emergency room after the incident. The doctor checked her blood sugar and gave her a pregnancy test, just in case. A few minutes later, the doctor told Eva she was expecting. After the doctor left the room, Eva went to Aaron.

She told Aaron, "I have something to tell you: I'm pregnant! We don't need Lisa after all.

We are going to have a baby." Aaron held Eva in his arms and smiled. He was in shock.

"I guess that's why you were so tired and not feeling well these last few weeks." Eva said, "Don't tell anyone until I'm ready, Aaron. Not even Rondell."

Eva just lost Diamond and on the same day she found out she was pregnant. Eva did not know how to feel. Eva had big plans for Diamond. She was going to help her get in college and get her nursing degree. Eva was concerned about Evan and who was going to raise him.

Aaron told Eva, "Don't worry about anything. Everything will work out." Diamond's mother was a strong woman and worked hard for her family. She knew she would raise Evan with her other five kids and make sure he was raised right. Eva was always pleased with how polite and kind Diamond's siblings were and how organized the house was. Aaron and Eva already agreed that they would take care of Evan's financial needs until he graduated from college. They would set up a trust for him as well.

Diamond's mother showed up at the hospital. It was too late. Diamond was gone. Her mother was hysterical. Aaron calmed her down and told her that Diamond was in heaven with God. "She's okay. You will be okay too. If you believe in God, you will see her again."

Nothing could comfort the mother of a child who just died. "If only she had her seatbelt on. That child never wore her seatbelt, Miss Eva!" Diamond's mother continued to cry. "Yes, she did, once. She wore her seatbelt when I drove her home from the hospital. I told her to always wear it." They embraced as Eva said she would help with the funeral arrangements.

Chapter 36

After Diamond's funeral Eva and Aaron waited a few weeks to tell their family and friends that they were expecting. They told Maria to plan a reveal party but not to let anyone know that it was a reveal party. Maria decided to tell everyone it was a white party.

The day of the party everyone showed up. Shawn Taylor showed up with a new girlfriend. Eva invited the Kellys and her close friends and family. It was a rainy day in Seattle when all the guests arrived. They ate dinner together, laughed, and Aaron played the piano for a little while. Everyone was happy. Suddenly everyone was called to the deck which overlooked the lake. The rain stopped right on time. Aaron thanked everyone for coming to the party and said, "Eva and I have a surprise for you all."

Maria rolled in a cake that was part blue and part pink. Aaron's mother covered her mouth, as she was in shock. "What does this mean?"

Eva looked at Aaron and they both said together in harmony, "We are having a baby!" Eva held her stomach and showed her bump. Julia Kelly screamed with joy. Col. O'Sullivan and Mr. Kelly pulled out cigars and embraced each other. "An heir to the throne."

Everyone wanted to know the gender of the baby. Eva and Aaron popped the white balloons that were hanging over the balcony and pink ribbons fell out. There were enough pink ribbons for every guest, with the name Diamond Daisy Whitfield O'Sullivan Kelly. Her nickname would be Deedee.

Everyone was thrilled. As the guests left the party everyone gave Eva and Aaron their best wishes. A few months later Eva and Aaron decided to have Thanksgiving dinner at the mansion in Salters, SC. They invited all of their family and friends and Nicolette and Ursula. As the guests arrived at the mansion the housekeeper gave them a gift and a room key. There were enough bedrooms on the estate to house all the guests.

Aaron and Eva took a trip to Charleston and arrived back home just as the last guest arrived. They pulled up in a chauffeured car. When they got out of the car Eva looked at the family cemetery from afar. She looked at the lake behind the house. Then she heard music. Someone was in the house playing Tchaikovsky's Symphony No. 6. Eva and Aaron walked hand in hand up the stairs to the front porch. Eva placed one hand on her stomach and looked at Aaron. Before they opened the door, they kissed passionately.

Eva and Aaron shared their traditional Thanksgiving dinner as they had in the past. Everyone enjoyed the meal, watched football, and Rondell and Aaron were trying to figure out where they would go Black Friday shopping. As Rondell and Aaron talked, Eva started a conversation with Nicolette. Nicolette looked at Eva's stomach and smiled. Eva said, "Is my baby going to be okay? I read that older mothers are at risk of having Down's syndrome babies."

Nicolette smiled and said, "You are going to have a healthy baby girl who is going to grow up and become an attorney. You have no worries, my child. You will see her graduate from college, marry, and you will have a grandchild. A boy. Eva, have you been having any dreams lately?"

Eva was shocked because she was having dreams about Evan and Diamond. "What are your dreams telling you to do?"

Eva said, "I don't know."

"Yes, you do. Look inside your heart. Listen to your mind. Listen to your soul. You know what to do."

Ursula just smiled. At first, they thought she was sleeping, as she held her head down often, as if she was napping. When Ursula looked up, she said, "My sister knows."

Eva hugged Nicolette and kissed Ursula's hand. "I've got to talk to Aaron."

When Eva found Aaron, she told him they should adopt Evan. She told him in her dreams, Diamond's mother was having a hard time raising six kids. "We should ask her if she wants us to raise Evan." She told Aaron that Diamond came to her in her sleep and told her to get him.

Aaron said, "If that's what you wish. You are his godmother. You were there when he was born. Let's make this happen. Our daughter will have a big brother. Now that's great."

Eva was so excited that Aaron agreed with her. Eva immediately called Diamond's mother, who agreed to let them adopt the baby boy. She knew he would have a great life with two loving parents. Later that evening, Eva and Aaron told all their guests that they were going to adopt Evan. "Cheers to that," said Colonel O'Sullivan. "I'm going to have a fishing buddy."

Rondell said, "I'm going to have a niece and nephew!"

Maria said, "And my new title is nanny!"

They all laughed out loud.

Eva said, "Not hardly. I will be a stay-at-home mom. I'll write books and motivational speeches, but my first job will be my husband and kids. But thanks, Maria, for volunteering. You'll still be my personal assistant." She winked.

The Monday evening following Thanksgiving, all of the guests packed up to leave Salters, SC. One by one, the cars filled up and drove off. Nicolette and Ursula were the last to leave. Nicolette moved back to Brazil to be with her sister. Rondell gave Eva and Aaron an early Christmas present, a painting for their home. The O'Sullivans said to hurry back to Seattle so they could plan a baby shower and get to know their new grandson.

Aaron's mother pulled Aaron aside and said, "You were right. Eva is a great person. She is your soul mate." She hugged her son and left.

Mr. Kelly said, "Aaron, congratulations. You are going to have a wonderful life."

"Dad, I already do."

"Yes. But wait until your daughter arrives. Your whole perspective on life will change."

He smiled at his dad and they shook hands and hugged.

After everyone left, Eva and Aaron reminisced about their life. Through their travel and experiences, they learned that there are six degrees of separation or maybe fewer social connections away from each other. They learned that everything happens for a reason, whether it's good or bad. They learned that although they were two decades apart, they were bound by love, faith, hope, and purpose. These quintessential virtues will drive anyone to find their divine purpose. Aaron thought about the first time they met. It was no accidental meeting. They were meant to be together.

Eva thought about meeting Nicolette and everything that she said was coming true. "Why did I take that selfie that day? Did I somehow know that I would meet her long-lost sister? Something just told me to take a picture!"

Aaron said, "What about your dad and my dad knowing Shorty? Now that was crazy!"

Eva began to reflect on Diamond. "Aaron, I told Diamond the day she took her baby home to always buckle up. She didn't. She died. I often wonder if I could have done more." Eva hung her head down.

Aaron said, "Eva, you were there when her baby was born. You helped her mother get that house together. She wanted us to be his godparents. It's tragic what happened to her, but you could not have stopped fate."

"Do you realize only a few minutes after Diamond passed, you found out you were expecting a baby? You ever wonder why that happened? That changed the narrative right away. Eva we began this journey looking for our divine purpose. I think we found it. We live to learn love. When we find that love, we share it. When we share it, the love spreads to the rest of the world. When there is love in the world, there is peace. When there is peace, there is harmony. If we live our life fulfilling our divine purpose, when our time comes for eternal life, we will be embraced by the light."

"Wow. So true my love." Eva looked at Aaron and said, "I wonder what her divine purpose is. She touched her stomach with her right hand and Aaron held her left hand as they walked back up to the mansion.

The sun was getting ready to set as they walked from the long driveway to the front porch of their majestic mansion. They watched the sun set on the lake while the trees with the moss blew in the wind. Eva kept Daisy's housekeeper to take care of the house. She knew Eva loved classical music so she played Tchaikovsky while Eva and Aaron watched the sunset.

It was a cool day in Salters, SC and the first day of the rest of their life together.

JUST LIKE YOU
By Theresa A. Moseley, Ph.D.

Happy hundredth birthday in heaven, Dad!

I know that you are my guardian angel.

I feel your presence all the time.

I am **JUST LIKE YOU!**

I joined the Army after high school,
JUST LIKE YOU.

I wanted to go Airborne,
JUST LIKE YOU.

I am creative and can sing,
JUST LIKE YOU.

I am kind and generous,
JUST LIKE YOU.

I care about world peace,
JUST LIKE YOU.

I am emotional and cry at the end of a great movie,
JUST LIKE YOU.

I have dry skin,
JUST LIKE YOU.

I like hot sauce,
JUST LIKE YOU.

I'm a great cook,
JUST LIKE YOU.

I am a forgiving person,
JUST LIKE YOU

I have a sense of humor,
JUST LIKE YOU.

I love to watch baseball,
JUST LIKE YOU.

I have a sense of style,
JUST LIKE YOU.

I wear hats,
JUST LIKE YOU.

I have that square jaw,
JUST LIKE YOU

I have eyes,
JUST LIKE YOU

I love music,
JUST LIKE YOU.

I love the ocean,
JUST LIKE YOU.

I love to watch the sunset
JUST LIKE YOU.

I will never forget the last time I saw you alive: my graduation from Georgia State University.

No one told me how ill you were, but somehow, I knew you were dying.

I was close to you emotionally and spiritually. I could feel your soul.

I KNEW! I always knew what you were thinking, when to call you, and how you were feeling.

I KNEW! I know you knew the same about me.

That's why you didn't have to worry about me when I was traveling the world.

The last time I saw you, you held my Bachelor of Arts Diploma in your hand

And told me how proud you were of me and that this degree was worth millions.

I will never forget that day. I watched you leave my house, and somehow, I knew I would never see you again in this life.

One day, when I have fulfilled my divine purpose, I will see you again, and I'll take my place as a guardian angel too.

JUST LIKE YOU!

Happy Birthday, Dad! I love you! - Resalee

About the Author

Theresa A. Moseley PhD is originally from Fayetteville, North Carolina. She is a United States Army Veteran, a member of the Screen Actors Guild, a central office school administrator, and a lifelong member of the National Association of Black School Educators (NABSE). She attended Georgia State University, Bowie State University, and The American University where she graduated with a PhD in 1998. In 2014, she published her first novel The Fourth Child: Five Decades of Hope, and in

2019 was a contributing author for Women of Virtue Walking in Excellence. Dr. Moseley is a motivational speaker, humanitarian, and a world traveler. She's lived in Augsburg, Germany and Sinop, Turkey. Her international travels include Great Britain, Italy, France, Spain, Australia Africa, New Zealand, Brazil, Morocco, Mexico, and Canada.

Dr. Moseley has worked in the field of education for 25 years. In 1999 she was awarded the Excellence in Education Award from the Prince George's County Chamber of Commerce. In 2006, she was recognized as Prince George's County Outstanding Educator. During her time as an assistant principal at Walker Mill Middle School, she received the Excellence in Gifted and Talented Education Award from the Maryland Department of Education.

She currently has a campaign for Creating Ambassadors of Peace: No More Violence, One School, One Community, One County at a Time. Dr. Moseley always has positive messages in her books about peace, love, hope, and purpose. She uses her life experiences to address thought provoking questions around finding one's purpose in life, finding your authentic self, and is very overt regarding everyone taking responsibility for creating a peaceful world.